THE MERMAID BRIDE

LIDIYA FOXGLOVE

Make sure you don't miss a release! Sign up for my mailing list.

🌸 Created with Vellum

Prologue

The Sea Witch

"Talwyn! Talwyn...!"

The witch heard the man calling from afar as he walked along the rocky shore.

He calls for Talwyn Silverfin? That girl was not the most conventional choice to capture a young man's heart, was she? But then again, Talwyn's bold eyes, her sun-kissed skin and hair—some wild youth would appreciate that more than a fair and dainty thing.

The bitterness had been with Rusa for so long that she relished it. She would punish this young land-dweller man, she thought, for dreaming of stealing a girl of the seas.

She swam below the surface of the water, skimming through the shallows near the beach, until she found the cluster of rocks the merfolk called the Hammer. She surfaced, feeling the sudden weight of all her jewels. She moved carefully up the rocks to peer out between their crevices and cracks, excited at the prospect of this trick.

The man walking the beach wore the crest of the royal family on his sleeve. Was this one of the high elven princes? It would not be the eldest, then. He had recently wed and likely would not be poking around the shore calling another woman's name.

No, this must be Prince Wrindel, the younger son—and a well-known rake.

"Talwyn, are you here? Where in blazes are you?" He picked up a shell and tossed it into the water.

Prince Wrindel was looking for a mermaid. And not just any mermaid. He knew Talwyn's name. They had spoken.

One of fate's little jokes? Here I am, back in Wyndyr...watching history repeat itself.

Rusa knew the ways of men. With his older brother wed, Wrindel must now find a bride himself. In such a position, he should not be looking for Talwyn. He should be courting a girl from the land.

But men always want what they can't have.

And maids are foolish enough to give it to them.

Rusa ran her knobbed old fingers over the rare shore-stone jewels hanging over her sagging breasts. She had just one left. Her mind cast back to a dark past, to the glitter of candles in mirrors, the rustle of silk dresses.

Rusa liked to grant men and maids their foolish wishes. Before she went to sleep, she listed their names as she ran her fingers over the empty settings of the jewels she had bargained for their lives. *Milsa. Selbia. Allawyn. Sumira.* Four shore-stones, four mermaids who would never know the ocean again. Curious little fools.

She clambered and heaved herself up the rocks, still strong despite her age. "Prince Wrindel?" she called. "Are you looking for someone?"

He glanced toward her. He didn't seem startled, which made her cross. She was no longer beautiful by any stretch of the imagination, so at the least, she liked to think she was startling. "Why, yes," he said, walking over. He had to look up at her, as she was perched on one the large boulders. "Greetings, maid. Do you know one of your kin named Talwyn?"

"I do," Rusa said. "I do indeed." Although she really didn't *know* Talwyn. She knew *of* her. But Rusa had a feeling most other merfolk would say the same about Talwyn. The Silverfin girls kept to themselves, and much like Rusa herself, they didn't stay in the same region for long. Some merfolk liked to settle in a placid little village; others were best suited to a wandering life. Rusa posed herself as a traveling healer, fixing the small wounds and sicknesses in a village. Talwyn Silverfin, meanwhile, was a scavenger, her presence tolerated more so than appreciated.

"I'm looking for her," the prince said. He paused. "She helped us slow down a ship a few weeks ago. I wanted to thank her, but I haven't seen her since." He glanced at the gold links around her neck, with the single shore-stone, the smoky gem that sat on her breastbone, the bangles flashing at her wrists. "Those are some beautiful jewels you have. I hope you aren't the sea queen, or I've been rude."

"No, I'm afraid I am not the sea queen," Rusa said. "I don't think there is a sea queen."

"Isn't there?"

"No, no, it would be hard to rule over such an untamed place as the sea. I am just a very old mermaid..."

"I get the feeling you're more than just that," he said, with an easy grin.

Damn pompous princes. He was trying to sweet talk her to get to Talwyn. He would never know how beautiful she had once been. "You want to thank Talwyn, do you?"

"Yes."

"Then...ah—poor girl. You do not know."

His brows furrowed. "Did something happen to her?"

"She smacked her head while she was helping with the ships. She was badly injured and has lost her memory." The lies came easily.

"No—truly? I don't believe it. She seemed fine that day."

"I'm a healer. Head injuries often don't manifest until the next day. She's a tough girl, of course; she didn't let anyone know she was hurt."

"Is there something I can do for her?" He rubbed his temple. Beneath a polite and easygoing veneer, she saw something else in his gray-blue eyes. Something firm and commanding. This was a man used to getting what he wanted.

"I don't know, good sir. She will probably be sent to the sick grotto, the place for mermaids who can't take care of themselves. If she gets her memory back soon, she can return to normal life... If not, well...I suppose that will be her home forever." Rusa crouched low on the rock, leveling her gaze at his. "The sea is far too dangerous for a mermaid with no memories. It is a shame, but fortunate that it happened before she married. At least she has no husband or children to worry over."

Prince Wrindel had a heart as gullible and hopeful as any man. *If only I had known earlier in life,* Rusa thought, *how easy it was to lie to them.*

"Bring her to me," Wrindel said. "She helped us. The elves can give her a safe home. The moat of the Palace of Waterfalls—"

"Is too small for a mermaid."

"My grandfather had a mermaid mistress," he said, in a voice that sent a chill down her spine.

"I didn't think anyone spoke of her anymore."

"You're right. They don't. But Father told me about it in private."

Rusa swallowed back a lump in her throat, twisting one of her bangles. "There is one way, but—"

"Tell me," he said. "I'm a prince. I can take care of a lot of buts."

"Oh, I'll bet you can," Rusa said. "Mermaid tails *can* change to legs..."

His eyes widened. "To legs?"

"It takes a great deal of magic to accomplish. I could do it."

"What is your price?"

She brushed her fingers across the hair that fell across his brow—fairer than gold. His hair was shorter than his predecessors, curling a little at the ends. But she remembered how soft and fine elven hair was. How it felt twined through her fingers. To his credit, he didn't cringe back from her.

"Oh, the things I could tell you about mermaids, Prince

Wrindel," she said. "Mating between two merfolk is quite straightforward and tidy. Most mermaids will never know the exquisite pleasures of a human form. Most mermaids will be admired by men like you only to a point before their tails are just a disappointment. Oh, Prince, if you captured young Talwyn in her first taste of a human form, you would be able to teach her *everything* of those pleasures."

He flushed handsomely, and he was such a beautiful man that for a moment Rusa wanted to change her mind. It wasn't worth giving Talwyn this kind of delight, even if meant stealing everything else from her, sentencing her to a lifetime of being torn between worlds.

Rusa brushed his forehead with her hand. She wanted to kiss him, every beautiful inch of his skin. She knew what he would look like under his clothes, pale and perfect, hard and soft, ready to claim his lover at a moment's notice. While the merfolk had a mating season, the land folk never went out of season.

To be young again!

She snapped her hand back. *Once a fool, always a fool*, she thought.

"I ask nothing," she said.

"You're a witch, aren't you?" Prince Wrindel said, stepping back. "You have that witchy way of talking." He raised an eyebrow. "Father told me never to trust witches."

"Why don't you see how good my word is? What do you have to lose, really?"

He tapped his fingers on the rock, assessing her with skepticism.

Rusa dragged herself closer to him, her tail heavy and useless outside of the sea.

He caught her hand in a tight grip. "You said it was difficult magic. Why would you grant me this favor?"

"Call me sentimental. I was young once. I know you won't be able to resist her, once she is yours. I like a happy ending."

"Damn it," he muttered. "I'm not sure what the catch is, but I know there is one. This is too good to be true."

"I suppose there is nothing I can say to change your mind. I think Talwyn cared about you. But she will never remember you now. You could make her remember, I'm sure."

He was still blushing. Men were very flustered by mermaids. Mermaids were undeniably attractive to men, with their pretty faces, full bare breasts, and lean swimmer's bodies. But they didn't want a woman with a tail. It drove them half crazy, to fall for a mermaid. She had seen it dozens of times.

A mixture of fear and rage rushed through her, remembering how it had all gone. Looking at this prince, it all seemed like yesterday. The attraction and the torment, with no good resolution... Why must the mermaids always be the ones to sacrifice?

She flashed him a smile that probably seemed forced. "I will leave you alone, Prince."

"Wait, I—"

She paused.

He shook his head. "No. Never mind. Go. Go on," he said forcefully.

The prince had more willpower than she had expected. But, no matter.

She had cast the bait, tempted him with a taste. The wheels of fate would repeat themselves, again and again. Soon, she would catch him, tempt him too far, and consign a bold young woman to a terrible fate. It would end in heartbreak, as it always did. And the best part about Talwyn Silverfin was, besides her timid little sisters, no one would care that she was gone.

Chapter One

TALWYN

THE DOCK WAS WELL LIT by the half moon, and there wasn't a soul around. Somewhere, I knew, a guard was prowling, but I saw no sign of him now. I paused for just a moment, intrigued by the vision of the human world. Everything was different above the water. Noisier, heavier, busier. Ships slowly bobbed at the docks, creaking and groaning at their moorings. The dock was stacked with crates. I smelled a whiff of smoke on the air. I knew I wasn't supposed to like it as much as I did.

I dove back under. "I don't see a soul around. Come on." I waved my sisters forward.

My sisters grinned, following me. It had been a while since we'd swiped anything right off the dock. The shipwreck over by the Wolf's Jaw had kept us busy during the summer. We gathered up every bit of scrap we could—at one point, using knives and harpoons to fend off a lone merman who tried to horn in on our loot. Then we carried the bounty down the shore and sold it to the land folk in the fishing villages in exchange for their food, drink, and dances.

There was nothing better than to watch the humans dance, the swirling skirts and stomping shoes, all the weird noises their instruments made. Their world was so strange, but I liked every taste of it I got.

We reached the dock. The waves slapped against the sea wall. The edge of the dock was out of reach, but once I surfaced, Allie spun her hook around and threw it onto the wood. She missed the first time, and cringed.

"I hope that wasn't too loud," she said.

"It's fine! Come on, you've still got the best throwing arm." Allie always needed some encouragement. She was a shrinking little fish if you didn't help her along.

On her second try, the hook caught the planks of the dock securely. Now we could climb the robe, hauling ourselves up hand over hand.

I always went first. I was the least afraid of getting caught, especially now. I could count one of the elven princes as a friend. If the guard spotted me here, I was sure I could talk my way out of it. Men of the land *never* suspected a mermaid of being a smuggler.

I dragged myself toward the stacked crates. A small, rectangular one caught my eye. It was stamped with four symbols, and I sort of recognized the shape of them. The land folk had an elaborate communication system called writing. Although I couldn't hope to truly understand it, I'd been doing this long enough that I recognized some of the combinations.

"This one," I said, pointing up at the little crate at the top of the stack. "Pins."

"You sure? It's out of reach," Mirella said.

"Pretty sure I recognize the symbols."

"You've been wrong about symbols so many times."

"Yeah, but the size is right too."

We were all sitting on the docks now, peering up at the crates which were stacked four high. If we had legs to stand on, we could have easily gotten to the crate. But on land, our tails were pretty useless. Of course, if it was easy to steal goods off of docks, wouldn't every mermaid do it? (Probably not. Most mermaids were pretty easily amused.)

"It's worth trying," I said. "You know how much we got from the last crate of pins! We could take that down to Vermon, stay there all winter, and drink wine."

Humans used a lot of pins. They went hand in hand with all of their clothes and hats. They even had to stick pins in their babies because human babies can't just piss any old place, but have to wear an elaborate configuration of cloth tucked around their bums. They were an easy trade for us, because we could sell a crate of pins even to a poor village, and unlike some other goods like cloth or food, they would hold up underwater for a decent length of time before they started to rust. Even other merfolk bought pins occasionally. So a crate of pins was about all we needed to buy ourselves some entertainment. We didn't need much, after all.

"Mm," Allie said. "But...you want to go to Vermon? You really want to leave Wyndyr?"

Allie was annoyingly perceptive. You couldn't keep a secret from her.

"Yes," I said, curtly. I knew what she was getting at, and I was trying with all my might to resist.

"But what about that man you keep talking to?" she pressed.

"I don't care. So we talked a few times," I said. My sisters didn't like going to the shore unless I prodded them, so they had never seen Prince Wrindel. I had been very vague, talking about him. It was, in any case, irrelevant. Whether he was a prince or a fisherman, I couldn't keep spending so much time with him. He was starting to look at me like no man had ever looked at me before, and I was starting to look at him too, and it was a bad idea all around.

"A *few* times?" Allie said. "You've been sneaking off all summer."

I ignored that. "Anyway, what is he going to do, marry a mermaid?" I scoffed. "Nah, it's time for us to move on and that's that."

"I bet we come back," Mirella told Allie. "Talwyn has a fancy for that human."

"He is a high elf, and I don't fancy him, and we are *not* coming back," I insisted. "What, do you want to encourage me?"

"No," Mirella said hastily.

"We've been worried about it, actually," Allie said. "But...it's really pretty here. I just thought— Maybe we could stay the winter, so you could keep talking to him and we could keep talking to our friends here."

"What friends?"

They started throwing names at me. "Kassia." "The man who sells the conchs, he talks to us a lot." "And Miss Ariand. She said she could use some help in her accessories shop."

One thing I had learned about managing my little sisters a long time ago is that I had to persuade them into doing what was best for them, and often that meant playing along until they came to their own conclusions. It was something my mother told me before she died. *Don't give people what they expect, give them what they really want.*

My sisters thought I would argue about leaving, but they wouldn't really like working in some boring shop. "Well, if you want to," I said. "I suppose we could all *work*. Settle down. It's very cold here, but it's true. I wouldn't mind talking to *that man* a little longer."

They looked at each other.

"Really?" Mirella said. "We could stay?"

"Really?" Allie echoed. "All winter?"

My brow furrowed. For once, this wasn't working. "Come on, girls, you don't *really* want to stay. In this boring place?"

"But why not?" Allie joined in. "You afraid we might actually make some friends if we stayed in the same place for a whole year?"

"I don't mind making friends," I said. "It's just—there are new places to see."

"Why do we always have to see new places? What's wrong with just seeing the same places? Maybe not everything is about places. Sometimes *people* are better than *places*," Allie said.

I was a little stunned at just how firm and mature she sounded in this moment. My shy little sister—she was a grown woman now, past her eighteenth year, even if it was hard for me to see her that way. And Mirella was turning seventeen.

I had a squirmy feeling in my gut that I didn't like at all. "You're telling me you don't want to travel anymore?"

"I don't know, Talwyn...maybe. For a little while, anyway..."

"We never really have liked scavenging," Mirella said. "It's just what we do to survive."

"'I don't know what sea crab got into your hair tonight," I said, bristling. "If you hate it so much, you could have told me."

"Not really..."

"This is a cold place to stay all winter," I said. "Warmer waters await. New friends, too. We just need something good for trading. C'mon, let's get out of here before the guards come prowling around. Help me." I reached upward to the edge of the first crate and pulled myself up. Taria wrapped her arms around my tail and helped support me to reach higher and then Allie came in too. My tail was pretty strong, but my fins didn't distribute weight in the right way to allow me to stand. Their arms helped support me in lieu of feet. The wooden crate at the top of the pile, which was stacked three deep, rested in easy reach.

Unfortunately, now my head was up close to a land-person level and I could see a guard swigging out of a bottle, leaning against a little building in the distance.

I got this weird little jolt, seeing the guard, because it was getting to the point where seeing any man at all made me think of Prince Wrindel.

I really needed to get out of here before I lost my head completely. I wouldn't be one of those silly mermaids they told stories about, who gave up her whole life to marry a man with legs.

"Guard!" I hissed. I tried to pick up the crate, but it was pretty heavy. "I'm giving it a shove into the water," I whispered. "Be prepared to grab it and go."

"I don't like this," Allie said.

I ignored her, giving the crate a good push. It slid off the pile toward the water. At the same time, I dove backwards off the other side of the dock. My sisters let go of me, slipping in after me. The crate was bobbing, sinking slowly. The pins were heavy but the wood wanted to float. Allie jammed her hook into the edge of the crate and we dragged it along with us, swimming away as fast as we could.

If the guard noticed us, we never knew. Once we were under-water, we were unlikely to be pursued. We yanked on the rope, dragging the crate under. A few bubbles emerged from the cracks around it as it started drifting down.

The salty water felt good on my skin. This world was weight-less and soft, my native element. We used a different pitch to our voices when we were under the surface, higher and more musical, so our words traveled. It was darker under the water, but my senses changed here, too. I saw the dim shapes of the rocks under the surface and the ocean floor, but I also heard obstacles from the way our voices traveled, and sensed things in the currents.

The merfolk said the ocean asked its children not to think, but to simply be.

As the years went by, I understood this more and more—not because I was good at simply being, but because every time I went to the surface, I started to think. And wonder. And ques-tion. Not just about things I was supposed to wonder about, like the beauty of a coral reef, or the meaning of the stars, but...other things. Things about the human world. What was it like inside their grand theaters, what use did they have for all their writing, and what were all their strange contraptions for?

This, the elder merfolk called "the Great Temptation". Dolphins and octopi were intelligent creatures too, but mermaids were the only creatures of the sea who were cursed with the ability to speak to the legged folk and the potential to be intrigued by their world.

A world where I knew I didn't really belong.

Wrindel spent a lot of time by the water. That was where I first noticed him, just standing on the shore, looking out at the endless gray water. There was something irresistible about him, from the first moment, seeing a man standing alone, right on the edge of my world. His boots were stripped off, his trousers rolled up to his knees, his feet crusted with sand, the wind whipping his hair into his eyes. That was how I would always see him.

"Talwyn, I don't know if there are pins in here," Allie said. "It doesn't feel as heavy as it should."

"We're far enough away," Mirella said. "We might as well check. It would be silly to keep lugging this crate if there isn't anything useful inside."

"Fine," I agreed.

Allie took another tool from the belt woven from fishing net she wore around her waist: a small prying bar. We stole useful tools from shipwrecks whenever we could, and used them until they rusted. Allie liked this part best. It was no wonder, I thought begrudgingly, that she wanted to work in an accessories shop, where she could carve shells, poke holes in things, and shape wires and netting. She loved working with her hands.

The crate had been sort of half-floating along with us. Mirella and I held it down as best we could, sending up small clouds of sand, while Allie pried up the edge.

She pulled out a small box, one of many inside nested in some shipping straw. The box was made of paper that was already starting to fall apart in her hands. Inside was a small cylindrical object with a silver pointed tip.

"Not pins," Allie said.

"That's obvious."

"What is it?"

"Maybe some sort of knife."

We surfaced to get a closer look.

"If it's a knife, it's very strange. It feels like it opens in the middle." I tried to open it. At first it wouldn't go, and then it snapped, and something like squid ink burst out onto my hands.

"It's an ink knife!" Allie said. "But...what for?"

We all paused, sensing the water move strangely around our tails, and ducked under the surface again—just in time for a net to suddenly sweep around my arms and face. I screamed, and

Mirella reached for me—only to snatch her fingers back as a flash of magic struck her.

My breath came in short gulps as I heard a woman's voice sing out behind me, "Talwyn Silverfin, your days of thieving are over."

Chapter Two

TALWYN

THE WOMAN JERKED the net toward her, bringing me with it as the tight, matted weave tangled me up even tighter. The more I fought, the more I seemed to get stuck in it. I tried to fight back with the strange knife-thing, or better yet, get the bone knife at my belt, but my arms were caught.

I saw Mirella and Allie in front of me holding their knives, clutching each other's hands, their long hair floating around them. It was too dark to see their faces well, but the moonlight filtered down into their hair in an eerie way. My little sisters... I couldn't bear to see them scared, and even less could I allow them to see *me* be scared.

But they had never been as bold as I was. Even now, they wouldn't go in a shipwreck unless I checked it first. They were afraid to see dead bodies or even skeletons. They weren't much for fighting either. Maybe I coddled them.

The woman swam close to me. I recognized her now. Rusa had come from the northern waters around the same time we traveled in from the south, and had offered healing services to the villagers here. Charms and curses, too, some people said, but I wasn't a villager, so I missed a lot of the gossip.

"Please," I said. "What do you want from me?"

"I want you as my prisoner. That's all."

"Why?"

"You're a thief. The staid village merfolk will never trust a scavenger, you know. No one will vouch for you. And you will never fit in here. You've caught the Great Temptation."

"That isn't true," I said, as I practically felt my sister's worry on the currents that surrounded us. They weren't moving. "Everything I do is for my family. My sisters and I lost our parents young, so we had to do something."

"You take your pickings and sell them to the land folk, don't you?"

"Yes..."

"What do you ask in return?"

I knew my answer would damn me. I asked for music, dancing, wine, a taste of their food. I asked them to throw us a party, and they made a fuss over us. Three mermaids was a thrilling excuse for a village to put on a festival, right there on the beach. "It's different," I said. "It's not the Great Temptation. We don't stay. We don't want to be a part of them."

"No," she said. "Prince Wrindel is your Great Temptation. And it works both ways. He is as tempted by you as you are by him, and he'll suffer for his desires, too. Don't worry. I won't hurt your sisters. The village will welcome them, with you out of the way. All I want is you."

Rusa was the kind of figure the merfolk told stories about to frighten their willful young girls into good behavior. How did she obtain all the jewels she wore? I had heard some of the village girls whispering about it. They said she traded with lords and princes for them. But just what did she trade?

"Please!" Allie cried. "Don't take her! Talwyn raised us! She's all we have! We don't trouble anyone; we just mind our own business."

"You're grown up girls. It's time you learned to handle yourselves. Settle down with a nice merman. Talwyn has done you no favors with all this mischief. Don't you dream of having friends and starting families of your own? You are tired of roaming the seas, aren't you? It gets old. I *know*."

Allie bit her lip. Horror rushed through me. Rusa had probably overheard them in the village, expressing their desire to stay. She was preying on them now, trying to turn them against me.

"What are you up to now?" Rusa smacked the crate with her palm. "Stealing pens?"

"'Pens'? What is that? How do you know?"

"I know everything. I'm a witch." She tugged on my net.

I struggled, whipping my tail around, trying to bust the net with my hands. Useless, but I had to try. "Wrindel wouldn't hurt me!" I said. "We're friends. He wouldn't fall for your tricks."

"He will," she said. "I have a plan to make you irresistible to him."

I managed to get my hand free between the net, and I reached for the first thing I could get my hands on: the necklace she wore. I yanked on it with all my might. My sisters rushed to my aid. Allie sawed at the net with her dagger. Taria slashed at her arm, nicking her skin. If this was the last I saw of my sisters, at least I could be proud.

Damnit, don't think it.

Rusa made a screeching sound at me, and she hissed spell words. Bubbly water rippled toward me. Allie turned to her with the knife, but I didn't see what happened. When the water hit my head, darkness fuzzed my vision. I thrashed, trying to hold onto consciousness, but it was no use.

WHEN I WOKE, I was chained up in darkness. I sensed the small room around me, with square walls. It must have been the interior of a shipwreck—probably a holding cell for prisoners on board. Merfolk homes were usually formed in caves or constructed with rocks, and were never so neatly built.

Shackles held my hands behind my back. I pushed my tail against the floor, holding my wrists straight, trying to slip free. The cuffs were tight.

I took a moment to calm myself and reflect. This might be the wreck we'd plundered last spring, in fact, when we first came to this region. I remembered it having a room where I found a drowned skeleton chained to the wall by his wrists and ankles. If so, she'd dragged me quite a ways.

"Rusa!" I shouted. "Where are you? This is a really dirty trick!"

She drifted down stairs, accompanied by a light-fish with glowing skin, and a shark for...well, I probably didn't want to find out what the shark was for. "Talwyn," she said. "Is there anyone who would miss you, besides your sweet little sisters? And they *are* better off without you. I don't think they really enjoy this vagabond life you're leading."

"My sisters are welcome to leave," I said. "But they love me, and I love them, and they'd rather stay with me. Our life is pretty exciting. I would think you'd understand. You're not one for settling down. You travel all over the realm yourself."

"Yes," the witch said. "But I am alone."

I couldn't tell if she was sad about that, or proud. She was hard to read, ancient as she was. Every inch of her face was lined with wrinkles. I had never seen a mermaid so old. The ocean was reasonably dangerous, so although mers could live almost as long as elves, it was rare to meet a mermaid who was facing her natural end.

Yes, Rusa must be near the end of her life, but she seemed so powerful that it was hard to believe. She was clad in an impressive amount of jewelry. The strangest piece was a necklace with gold settings to hold jewels, but only one stone remained: a milky blue-green colored gem. And the there was the heavy black jewel that kept luring my eyes. It gave me a shiver whenever I looked at it, for some reason, as if it held dark power. She came closer to me. I cringed back as reached for my face. Her fingernails scraped my cheek as she touched me.

Her thumb popped something in my mouth. I hadn't realized

she was holding anything, and it took me by surprise. It was small, hard, and round, like a little polished pebble. She immediately covered my mouth with her palm so I couldn't spit it out.

"Swallow it," she said.

"Nn-nn."

"You can swallow it, or I can make you swallow it."

The shark circled. I glanced around. *There must be a way out of this.* There was a way out of everything, right?

But between the shark, and the shackles, and the fact that she had magic... I'll admit it. I was afraid things could only get worse.

Maybe it meant I wasn't as brave as I thought I was, but I swallowed the pebble. I felt it sliding down my throat, hard and unpleasant. "What is it?" I gasped as she removed her hand.

"It's a spell, naturally," she said. "I'm sorry for this part, I really don't enjoy it myself, but this is not easy magic, as I told Wrindel. Everything that makes you a mermaid has to go into that stone."

"What does that mean?"

"After the stone passes through you, its magic will have seeped into you, and your magic into it, and—"

"You're going to make me crap out that stone?"

"Well, where else do you think it's going to go?"

"You're disgusting."

She shrugged. "I heal people, dear. I've seen and done much more unpleasant things than that. Don't pretend to be prissy. I know you'd pluck a treasure right off a bloated corpse if I put one in front of you."

"I can't believe *anyone* would let you *heal* them. You just kidnapped me. Why would you do anything nice?"

"Well, we're not that different, are we? Everyone knows about you Silverfin sisters. You wait for shipwrecks. You pilfer things from the dead. You fend off other scavengers with knives and spears. You steal crates off docks. Are you nice?"

"I don't make the shipwrecks happen. I don't hurt anyone, not unless they hurt me."

"Stealing things hurts someone. You know that. You think

petty crime is charming, don't you? Rather rebellious? Why do you steal things? What is your aim? You want something in the end. You get a little amusement from the humans, a few trinkets, perhaps? No, I can't feel sorry for you. Although I do like you more than I expected. You remind me of myself more than any girl I've bargained off."

"I bet you say that to all the girls."

Rusa grinned broadly. Despite her age, she still had most of her teeth. "You're right. I do. But I do like you more than most. The thing is, the more I like you, the more I like selling you. I'm cruel, dear. Maybe some day you shall see, it's more fun to be cruel than anything else. Once you learn the satisfaction of cruelty, it will never disappoint you."

My face felt tight with tears. Luckily it was easy to hide tears underwater. All I had ever wanted to do was make my little sisters happy.

Okay, maybe that wasn't true. Maybe I was selfish. Maybe they would have been happier if we settled down in one village, made more friends, found contentment. But certainly, I might be a thief, but I had never been cruel.

"I don't think you answered my question," I said. "Why would you heal people when you'd rather be cruel?"

"Because, it gives me value. It lets me call in favors. It means no one will stand up to me when I get rid of you, because I mean more to them than you do."

That stung. Badly. Because deep down, I knew no one really loved me except my sisters, and I had no one to blame but myself. I was always chasing something I could never find, instead of being content with what was around.

Wrindel was the first person I had chased who had also stuck with me. Week after week, he kept coming to talk to me. At first, it was a light flirtation. Pretty soon, I was telling him everything: about how it was raising my sisters when I was only five years older, how I felt like their mother and yet so undeserving of replacing our real mother, about my travels, my wildest and silliest dreams.

"Wrindel won't want to trap me on land," I said.

"He will think he's doing you a favor," Rusa said. "You see, this spell will take away all your memories of your mermaid life. You won't know where to turn. You won't know where you belong. Prince Wrindel is actually the one who will steal the stone and your memories with it, but he won't know. He thinks you have amnesia. He will offer you a home. By the time he realizes what he has done, he will have a hard time letting you go." She paused. "In some ways, despite it all, I envy you."

"Why?"

"You will see many beautiful things, I have no doubt, before he gets bored of you... It might almost be worth it. Yes...my dear...it might be worth it."

Rusa was a very strange woman. I couldn't tell, in that moment, if she wanted to punish me...or live through me.

I was still shaking. Could she really do this? Could she take my memories away?

"You've seen it?" I asked, around my rising dread. I felt like that pebble was still stuck somewhere in my chest.

"I've seen it, but you will go farther than I did. I never had legs."

"You've been to the land?"

She looked at me with a heavy gaze, her eyes still large and clear. "You won't remember any of this," she said. "Yes, child. Once, I went to the land..."

Chapter Three

WRINDEL

MY FAVORITE COURTESAN was taking my cock out of my trousers, and yet, quite possibly this was the worst afternoon of my life. She wasn't cheap, the royal coffers were low anyway, and I didn't even really want to be here.

What the hell are you doing?

Distracting yourself?

Then I thought wryly, *Story of your life.*

"Mmm...prince...I've missed you." Deera looked up at me through a fringe of dark eyelashes. I looked at her and realized, that for all the times I'd seen this girl, I didn't actually know her at all.

"I shouldn't have done this," I said flatly.

"Nonsense." She slid her tongue up and down my shaft. I was getting hard, but more due to her skill than my own engagement. I leaned a hand against the wall. *Come on. You already paid, and...*

Imagine Talwyn doing this...

Her face sprung to mind immediately. Easy grin, tanned skin, dark blonde hair with surface strands kissed by the sun to a lighter shade, comfortable in her naked skin, with a rather direct way of speaking. I noticed something new about her every time we met. Last time, even though I'd been in the middle of trying to organize the merfolk to halt a ship before it got far from land, I noticed that she chewed her nails. They were all uneven and ragged and for some reason I found it charming.

She lived in a very different world from me, but you'd never know it, to talk to her. She didn't seem like some mythical siren, like the stories. She could have been a shepherdess or a girl selling peanuts on the corner, just far more interesting.

But—had she really injured herself that day?

I thought the witch was lying, but I also hadn't seen Talwyn since, and I was starting to go a little crazy. I needed someone like her, someone I could talk to who stood apart from all the worries swirling around the palace.

"Stop," I said.

"Stop?" Deera pulled back incredulously. "What's wrong?"

"I can't do this."

"Aw." She stood up and ran a hand through my hair. "Sweet Wrindel. You're worried about your father, aren't you?"

"Of course. I'm not heartless." It was easier to blame my sudden lack of interest on that. A few weeks ago, it looked like our kingdom might have happiness again, when my older brother Ithrin announced his engagement to an adorable half-goblin girl. But then my father had his 'spell'. He seemed confused as dinner began, and then he collapsed. The healers rushed to him, and pulled him through whatever it was for the moment, but he seemed out of it ever since. He kept getting dizzy and forgot things. Every day he grew weaker. He wasn't even getting out of bed now.

My father was young for a high elf, to face death. But ever since my mother and older siblings died when I was a baby, he didn't care much for his health. I guess it might have caught up to him.

My father seemed invincible, until this week.

"He's recovering nicely," I said, remembering to take the official stance. The people of Wyndyr knew he wasn't feeling well, but no one knew how bad it was.

"There's no shame in pleasure," Deera said. "You need to take care of yourself."

I shook my head. "I don't suppose I could...put it on hold for later?"

"Sure you can. You're my favorite customer." She sauntered to the side table and poured me a drink. "But are you going to be able to button your trousers? Your head might not be in it, but tell it to that stiff rod." She came over, sliding a hand up my shaft.

I cleared my throat. "Deera. I told you to stop."

She paused with surprise and maybe even a bit of pique. Then she handed me the drink with a shrug.

I took a swig of sweet wine. "A cold walk on the shore will straighten out my head. That's what I need right now. I'm sorry, Deera, you know it's not you. You're the loveliest woman in Harborside."

"Once you told me I was the loveliest woman in Wyndyr. Now I've been downgraded to the neighborhood! Is it because Ithrin finally got married? How many hearts will break if you decide to grow up, Wrin? It'd be a national emergency."

"Yes," I said soberly. "But I suppose it would have to happen sometime."

As I left the tavern, I had this weird feeling I would never cross its door again.

I can't believe I've gotten wrapped up in one woman, I thought, taking the steep steps down to the rocky shore. It was getting closer to sunset, and our city faced to the west, so I thought I'd stroll long enough to watch. *A mermaid, at that.*

This was her world: the dark mystery of the water. It was not a place for me, and my world was no place for her either. If she was an ordinary girl, I told myself, I would've forgotten her already. I was obsessed because I couldn't have her, that was all.

But what if I'd always known? The sea was the place I turned to when I felt especially lost, even when I was a boy, long before I could turn to women. I used to spend hours picking my way along the rocks, looking for treasures, letting the waves ebb and flow around my bare feet, gazing at the unknown. This was the place I found peace, and it made some sense that a girl from the sea would be the girl I couldn't forget.

Wyndyr had always lived and died by the sea. Like all the kingdoms of the Isles, we were a hub of trade and fishing. Every person in the city knew the signs of an approaching storm. Today, it was calm. I stood there for a little while, hands in my pockets, cold wind whipping my hair into my eyes. The waves tumbled onto the beach in a rhythm. Farther out, fishing boats were steady as they sailed back to the harbor before sunset.

Despite the cold, I took off my shoes, like I always did as late into the fall as I could stand, hooking my fingers around the laces of my boots. I started walking again, passing children who were looking for mollusks. They waved at me, most of them too young to recognize their prince.

I stopped short when I saw something in the distance, on the rocks where I had recently encountered the witch.

Was that a body sprawled on the boulder?

I started running, rocks jabbing the soles of my feet.

Yes. It was a mermaid. She wasn't moving.

"Talwyn?" I caught my breath as I reached her, after a long sprint. "Tal!" She was slumped on the rock, unconscious, but breathing. Thank the stars for that. Her hair was almost dry, like she'd been there a while. The skin of her tail was almost dry too. I wondered if she was all right like that, or if her tail needed to stay wet. It was smooth silver-gray, like a dolphin, but more luminous. Seeing her like that made me think of a fallen star.

"Talwyn?" I put a hand on her shoulder. Her skin was cold. I had never touched her before. Come to think of it, of all the lovely young women I'd spent time with, I don't think I had ever gone so long just talking, not touching.

Which meant I'd talked to Talwyn more than most women. It was strange to see her *not* talking. You know how some people just seem invincible? Talwyn was one of those people. It disturbed me to see her knocked out, like some law of the

25

universe had been broken. I suppose I should be used to that by now, after what happened to Father.

Around her neck hung a chain with a blue-green stone wrapped up with a gold wire. I had never seen her wear it before, and found it rather conspicuous. I reached for the stone—and heard a whistle.

The witch-mermaid from before surfaced in the water just below the rock.

I stood up and drew the slender blade I carried. "What did you do to her?"

"Isn't she beautiful?" the witch shouted to me, her voice melodious and younger than her face. She wasn't that far away, but the waves striking the rocks made for a lot of noise. "It's your decision, but just so you know, if you take off the necklace, her tail will split into legs. You have to hide the stone from her and never say a single word about it. If she so much as lays an eye on it, if you even tell her you have hidden it from her, she will immediately become a mermaid again. And this time, it will be forever. Maybe your healers might be able to help her amnesia in a more natural way. Who knows?"

I knew the witch expected something out of me. Maybe she had even cast an enchantment that would force me into loving Talwyn, the way my brother had initially been enchanted by his bride. I had encouraged Ithrin to give in to a love spell, but then, my brother was stiff around women. I didn't need such encouragement.

But whatever game the witch is playing, can't I outwit her?

I shouldn't make that assumption. But I also couldn't imagine leaving Talwyn behind, vulnerable to a woman with dubious motives.

Witches tended to cast their spells toward a man's weakness. And I certainly knew my weakness. My reputation probably preceded me. Even mermaids knew I couldn't resist a pretty face. She thought I wouldn't be able to handle a pretty face without legs, and the treasure between them.

I'll bloody well show her.

"I don't think I need to turn her into a land dweller to try and solve her amnesia," I said, taking Talwyn into my arms.

"That is true...," the witch said. "You are a kind man, after all." She bowed her head, seeming to indicate that she wouldn't stop me.

I carried Talwyn up a rugged path cut between stubby bushes heading back up from the shore to town. Talwyn was surprisingly heavy. Her body was long and felt more muscular than the idle society girls I was used to, and her tail kept bumping against the shrubs. She remained unconscious, one arm dangling down.

I stopped at the top of the path and took off my jacket, wrapping it around her naked breasts to shield her before I moved on.

Soon, I had reached a wooden promenade that fronted the beach, with painted clapboard cottages lining a well-kept lane. The men were still out fishing and the older children were mostly at school. I smelled bread baking. A lithe young elf-wife carrying a pail paused to stare.

"A mermaid," she breathed. Then, louder, "Is she hurt?"

"I don't truly know," I said.

"She'll only get sicker outside the water," the girl said, putting down the pail and walking over, wiping her hands on an apron. Then she stopped short and bowed. "Your highness! I didn't recognize you from a distance. You're taking her to the palace, then?"

"Yes," I said. "But what do you know about mermaids? Her tail is somewhat dried out. Is that all right?"

"Can I touch her?" the girl asked, hesitating before getting too close to me, her pale cheeks blushing. No doubt, she knew my reputation too. I flustered all the peasant girls. In the past, I would have gladly flirted with the young woman. Right now, my reputation was getting in my way. I didn't give a damn about anything except Talwyn.

The girl ran a hand along Talwyn's tail. "Your highness," she said. "Far be it from me to advise you, but she is quite dried out. She could catch sick. The merfolk really don't fare well outside the sea. Even the palace isn't a good place for her. The pools are shallow and the water is fresh. They can adapt to fresh water, but they don't thrive."

I hated to believe her, but the people who lived on the water knew more about merfolk than anyone else. "I can't put her back in the sea. She's a friend of mine, and she's hurt."

The girl glanced at me apologetically. "Her own people can help her better than we can. But—I could ask Dame Biriel, if you'd like to be sure. She's older than me, so—"

"I believe you," I said. "No need. I've had enough of old women today. Truth be told, I think there's a sea witch who has it out for her. The witch told me if I took off her necklace, her tail would turn to legs, and as long as I hid it from her, she could stay here forever. I could try it, and give it back to her once she's feeling better, if it's true. Have you ever heard of that sort of magic?"

"Oh yes," the girl said. "Of course. Some merfolk carry a talisman that lets them turn to human form. Some of them can't resist the land, you know, and the men dream of finding them. If a man steals it off her, she has to be his bride. That's the story I hear, mind you."

So much for my willpower. *I'll only keep the stone until she's feeling better,* I told myself. "Would you help me?" I asked. "I have to give it a try. If she's going to change forms, I'd need to borrow a dress from you for her to wear. I'll compensate you many times over."

"Oh, of course! Your highness, it would be my honor. But—" She flushed again. "I must get Dame Biriel. If my husband came home, she would—help me explain."

I knew what she meant. She didn't want her husband to find me alone with his wife. *Of all the stupid things.* "Hurry."

"She lives right next door to me!" The girl dashed toward one of the houses.

In another moment we had: Talwyn in bed in front of a crackling fire, me, the pretty young elf-maiden, a very vigorous older woman with a baguette tucked under her shoulder, and two small children arguing over a wooden horse. That was just how everything was in the hamlets lining the shore. Everything had an audience.

Dame Biriel had already taken the liberty of wrapping Talwyn's tail in a wet sheet, deftly handling this entire operation without dislodging the baguette, which I considered might taste of armpits by the time it was eaten. It certainly did make you think about food purchased on the street.

Talwyn still slept. No doubt, magic guided her slumber. No normal circumstance would allow a person to sleep through this ruckus. At this point, I was getting agitated. I just wanted to see her eyes open. I unfastened the necklace's clasp. Immediately, a spasm ran through her body, almost knocking off the wet sheet.

"Put it away," Dame Biriel told me, patting the necklace. "Quickly now. I knows the legend of the shore-stones. If you want her as a bride, you can't show it to 'er."

"He doesn't want her as a bride," the younger woman said. "He just wants to help her."

"Nonetheless, young man, put it away. She can't be seeing it now."

"Dame Biriel, this is the prince," the elf-maid said.

"I know he's the prince!"

"Oh, please do be polite, that's all."

I shoved the necklace in my pocket, barely paying attention to them. I was riveted by what was happening. Small moans escaped Talwyn's lips, and as she thrashed, her tail split into legs. Her fins shrank so quickly and naturally beneath the sheet, it was like watching a bellows deflate. The young woman finally nudged the children out of the room as Talwyn cried out like she was in pain. I clutched her hand. And then she kicked off the sheet.

Damn.

I already knew mermaids had the best breasts in the world, and Talwyn especially—full, round, and high, like they helped her float. Granted the miracle of legs, she had the most breathtaking form I had ever seen. A girl of the land, but—not quite. I had never seen a girl who looked so sleek, lean muscle and gorgeously formed ample curves, with the smoothest, softest skin you could imagine and not a hair on her anywhere besides her head. Her sweet little sex was plain to see and begging to be tasted.

I already knew I wasn't going to give her back up to the ocean easily. Maybe the witch had me. I didn't even care. It hit me hard. *I already love this girl.*

"Talwyn?" I said.

Her hand suddenly gripped mine back as her eyes flew open. She looked at me, at the two women, and at her body, and screamed loud enough to call the fishing boats into the harbor.

Chapter Four

TALWYN

I CLUTCHED the hand of a stranger. Strangers, everywhere. Every *thing* was strange. I was on land—*inside* of a house.

"Where am I?" I screamed, in a blubbering panic. "What happened to me? I'm a mermaid—I'm a mermaid—I can't remember anything."

"Shh, dear." An older woman patted my hand. "You're all right now."

"This is Prince Wrindel. He'll take good care of you," a younger woman said.

Prince Wrindel? I was hyperventilating, but I managed to stop screaming. Something about Prince Wrindel seemed...*sort of*...familiar.

I certainly hoped he was familiar, because he was absolutely gorgeous, and as scared as I was, that fact still didn't hurt.

Everything else was strange beyond words. I was disoriented, my mind reaching for something it knew was there but couldn't find. My memories were a haze. Instead of a tail, I had legs. Human legs. Human everything. I had been thrashing but once I realized this I went completely still and hugged my legs together. It frightened me, seeing them.

Wrindel pulled the sheet over me. "Talwyn...do you remember anything?"

"Not really! I remember my name. I know I'm a mermaid. It's all—vague."

"You lost your memory. I'm going to take you home and explain all that I know. Don't worry." He put a steady hand on my shoulder. "I'll take care of everything for you and make sure you get your memories back. All right?"

I nodded, somewhat dumbstruck. What else could I say? I didn't even know where I belonged, except under the water.

"I'll get you a dress," the younger woman said, opening a small cabinet with clothes inside.

I had only seen human rooms in shipwrecks, which meant I felt them in the shadows almost as much as I saw them. So in some basic way, this place felt familiar, but I had never seen a fire crackling softly in a hearth, or felt bed clothes around me, or been able to observe the details of furniture, curtains, and the way the light fell through the window. I couldn't decide whether it was nice, or deeply disconcerting.

"This is the best I have," the girl said, bringing over a green gown. "I'm sorry it's not much, your highness. I do think it will fit."

"Don't worry about that," Wrindel said. "It's perfect. Hold out your arms, sunshine."

I did, and he pushed the sleeves onto my arms. He seemed pretty relaxed, like he knew what to do, and I just went along with it as he tugged my head through the collar. I pulled it down over me the rest of the way. It was tight on me, and I felt trapped. Like I was wearing a net. I pinched and pulled at the fabric. But I realized the other women were dressed similarly. I suppose I just wasn't used to wearing clothes.

"There," he said. "Can you walk?"

"Walk? I don't know how to *walk*."

"I has a horse I can loan you," the older woman said.

"Very good. I want to get her somewhere safe and quiet as

soon as possible," he said. "Thank you, ladies. You've both been so helpful." He gave them each a few coins and they flushed and beamed, even the older one. My first thought was that I didn't like the way the young elven maid looked at him.

I clutched my head.

I felt like I was in some strange dream where none of my circumstances or emotions made any sense.

The young woman tried to offer me something to eat, which I refused, and something to drink, which I accepted. It was good ale, and helped calm my nerves a bit. A horse appeared outside. It poked its head in one of the open windows. The young woman laughed. "There is your ride, dear prince. Thank you so much."

"You've nothing to thank *me* for," he said. "I am grateful to you for helping me rescue my friend." To me, he said, "I'm going to carry you out of here, put you on the horse and bring you home. Then, we'll sort it all out. I'll get the healers to look at you. We'll get your memories back."

"Do you suppose I could take that ale with me?" I asked the young woman.

"Of course!" She gave me the entire skin.

Wrindel grinned at me. "There's a girl," he said.

Yes, whoever he was, he did know me. It was strange to have emotions for someone you didn't remember, but I did. He said I was his friend, and I sensed the edge of more. He was protective of me and I felt a little possessive of him. We couldn't have been lovers...no, not a mermaid and an elven prince. But he had reason to care for me, and that was the only thing I had to cling to right now.

The surface world was full of things I think I had heard of, or perhaps seen in other contexts, but I was pretty sure I'd never been in the middle of a town before. A lot of people were gathered around. A few of them greeted the prince, but mostly they were quiet, just politely snooping. He lifted me onto the horse and I suppressed a wave of terror at how big the creature was and that I had to split my legs to sit on it. It felt so wrong to have legs, like I had broken into pieces. The horse snuffled and moved slightly. I gripped the saddle in terror, afraid to move in case I upset it somehow.

Wrindel mounted behind me and settled me back against his chest. Clearly, he knew what he was doing.

The skin of my legs was exquisitely sensitive. A few minutes ago, it had not even existed, at least not in this form. Human skin seemed more fragile than my tail, and it was very strange to have such fragile skin surrounding such important parts of me. Between my legs, I was especially sensitive. As the horse walked, the leather saddle rubbed against me in a way that made me squirm. Paired with the arm of this strangely familiar and very attractive man at my waist, I had to squelch a wave of unexpected desire.

I'm not supposed to be enjoying this!

"You had me worried," he said, spurring the horse on down the street. I tensed at the movement, and he held me closer still. "You're steady," he said. "Not used to this, are you?"

"*No*. None of this."

"The last time I saw you, you were helping me track down a ship," he said. "I wondered why I hadn't seen you since. Then, they told me you'd lost your memory."

"How?"

"You hit your head."

"I can't believe I would hit my head!" I was indignant at the very idea. I had never been clumsy. I might not have my memories, but I knew my own self.

"Anyone can make a mistake..." But he sounded like he found it an odd story as well. "Do you remember anything?"

"No..."

"Something happened. I don't trust that old mermaid, but we'll figure it out."

"You keep saying that, but...*how* will you figure it out? Who is this woman?"

As we rode, he told me that he had met an old mermaid on the shore who told him of my condition, and that later she had brought me to him. The Palace of Waterfalls grew closer with every beat of the horse's hooves. I had never seen the palace up close, but it was unmistakable—and beautiful. So beautiful that I almost missed a chunk of his story, even though it was so important.

The palace was the perfect marriage of natural rock, surface construction, and water. It had been built into the side of a hill and was several stories tall, with small waterfalls spilling into pools on every level, ending in a moat at the bottom. It was very symmetrical, with neat rows of tall glass windows—so different from the natural caves and rocks that formed our homes. The light was clear today and smelled of bread and spices; the sun glinted on the waterfalls as the sky turned pink from the sunset. I had some idea of what this world was like, but it was always from the shore. I had never been in the midst of it before.

"You've always wanted to see it," he said. "You told me so. I know you were trying to pretend you didn't care that much that you couldn't travel on land. But you're here now, so you ought to enjoy it."

"How long have we known each other?"

"Should I tell you how we first met?"

"Of course!"

"Well..." He leaned back in the saddle a bit, but his hand remained at my hip, comfortingly solid through the thin fabric of my dress. "All my life, I've taken walks on the shore when I need to be alone. I think it was in the spring when I first saw you sitting there, picking bits of things off the beach. You told me you hadn't been in this region for long, and that you travel around looking for treasures. You aren't the first mermaid I've ever gotten conversational with, but..."

"But?" I prodded.

He hesitated, and then shrugged. "Well, I went to the trouble of saving you today, so there must be something about you."

"How often have we talked?"

"Not often enough. I'm lucky to see you once a week. Of course, mermaids don't have clocks, and princes can't spend all their time wandering beaches hoping to run into them."

"We've spoken once a week since spring? It's autumn now."

That was more than enough time for courting, if we had been the same species.

"Yes…"

"That's quite a lot of visits we've had."

"My family had no idea I was meeting a mermaid down there. Of course, my family doesn't know half of what I'm up to. But I'm going to have to explain you now."

"Explain me?"

"You'll have to live in the palace for a little while. But it's a pretty nice place."

We were right at the foot of the building now. My eyes cast upward, taking in details: fish carved into eaves, colored tiles decorating the wall under an open walkway. Even the stone channel that the moat water spilled out of was carved on the end into a shape like flower petals unfurling. I had the sense that I wasn't supposed to be admiring the surface world as much as I did. I was supposed to tell myself I didn't belong here.

I could hardly wait to see the rooms inside.

"A 'pretty nice place'?" I said. "If only the merfolk could build such dwellings."

"Well, sunshine, every place gets boring after a while," he said. He led the horse into an adjacent building to the palace. I could smell the livestock from a distance. Inside, dozens and dozens of stalls held as many horses in an enormous room that smelled of hay and dung. I wrinkled my nose. The ocean currents kept waste from being a problem.

He dismounted and helped me down into his arms, and I felt like I was made of knees and elbows.

"I've got you," he said.

I was going to make a joke about the horse shit, but the way he looked at me put the world on pause.

"I've always wished I could show you this place, at least once," he said.

I felt as if I had dreamed of being here with him, too—even as I suspected that this was a terrible, hopeless thing to dream. Mermaids didn't belong here. Every minute I spent in this place, I was leaving something important behind. I just couldn't remember what it was. With every passing moment, it seemed to matter less.

My eyes drank in the sight of him, eyes full of humor and... need. Yes. I saw it there. He desired me; he had been dreaming of this. I had never been close to a merman, but an elven man was quite different in any case. Everything on land seemed more solid and important and dangerous—including the people. It stirred my curiosity.

"Talwyn...," he said, his voice low, like a caress on my ear.

My heart was beating so fast I was sure he could hear it. *Don't you dare,* I told myself. *You need to get your memories back and go home, and if you entangle yourself, it will only make it harder to do what must be done.*

"Wrin?"

When another male voice called out behind us, Wrindel shifted his grip on me. I went from 'rescued girl' to 'sack of grain'. Clearly he didn't want to get caught being too intimate with me. "Ah," Wrindel said. "This is Talwyn. I need to see if the healers can help her. Seems she has a little amnesia."

"Is this the mermaid you were talking about?" The other man bore a strong similarity to Wrindel. His fair hair was a little longer, his eyes darker, his body a little more tall and lean, but I wasn't surprised when he said, "I'm Ithrin. Wrindel's older brother."

"Yeah, I did mention her to you once, didn't I?"

"Yes." Ithrin lifted an eyebrow. "A little amnesia? How does one get 'a little' amnesia?"

"She hit her head."

"Sounds like magic."

"I don't know, that's why I want to take her to the healer. But first I just want her to have a chance to rest. She's not used to our world."

Ithrin flicked a gaze at me and then back to his brother again. "Can I talk to you for a moment, Wrin?"

Wrindel scowled at his brother. "Not now." He started walking briskly toward the door. "How is Father doing?"

"No change, for better or for worse, but I suppose that's good enough for now. His mood has improved; at least, he's been teasing the maids, although he did ask for a gods' blessing again this morning."

"Good enough for now," Wrindel agreed, but he sounded grim. "I'll see you at dinner."

"But—wait—"

"At *dinner*," Wrindel insisted. "I'm obviously busy."

"You be careful with him!" Ithrin told me as Wrindel hustled me up a narrow staircase.

"Ignore him," Wrindel said. "He's always trying to tell me what to do."

"Siblings can be like that," I said, memories pricking me. I had siblings, didn't I? It was very distressing that I couldn't remember any family at all. "Your father isn't well?" I asked.

"He's...recovering. He'll be fine." I could tell he didn't want to talk about it, and it was easy to put it all out of my head as he carried me into the main interior of the palace. The room opened up like a vast cave, only no cave could ever be as beautiful as this. Stone walls soared into arches, with clear glass windows on our eye level and colored ones up high. The golden light of sunset played in huge shapes on the floor and caught the sparkling water in rows of square pools. It was very strange to see water placed in such orderly containers, each one with a statue in the middle, water burbling up around the carved forms of fish and mermaids.

I looked over his shoulder and then twitched in his arms, wanting to look closer. I wished I knew how to walk, but it also stirred some childish instinct to play in the water, the way I used to when I was little.

The hall was fairly empty and quiet. A few elven ladies were strolling arm in arm, speaking in soft voices to one another, glancing at Wrindel with polite curiosity.

"I'll introduce you later," he said. "Let's get you somewhere quiet first, sunshine."

"Who told you you could call me 'sunshine', anyway?"

"You did. When we first met, you didn't want to tell me your name. I asked if I could call you 'sunshine' because your hair. It's not as naturally fair as mine, but it shows that you've been kissed by the sun. You said it would be all right. You wrinkled your nose a bit. Nobody calls you pet names back home, I guess?"

"I guess not."

"Eventually, you did tell me your name, but by then, it was a habit."

I don't think anyone ever pays this much attention to me, I thought.

He passed through the hall, to a smaller but still airy corridor. The palace seemed vast, and every inch of it continued to be lovely and unfamiliar to me. I could hardly fathom the wealth and resources the royal family must have, to own all this. A damp chill pervaded the stone walls. Despite the beauty, I'm not sure it was the most comfortable dwelling.

He nudged open a door with his shoulder, finally carrying me into a bedroom. Bedrooms were another thing I had only seen on shipwrecks. Many ships had just one bedroom for the captain, some had several, and otherwise they contained hammocks or bunks. The bedrooms were the nicest spots on the ship, the best rooms for plunder outside of the cargo hold, and particularly eerie underwater: bed curtains and sheets softly floating in the shadowy waters, rooms full of the personal effects of their (usually dead) inhabitants.

This, for some reason, I did remember.

He put me down on the bed and then he took the skin of ale from me. It had been resting on my lap and I'd almost forgotten I had it. He poured some into a glass and handed it to me. "That'll warm you up until I get a fire going," he said. "It's cold in here."

"Mermaids don't...really get cold," I said, but as soon as I said it, I realized I was actually shivering.

"We poor land people do," he said, pulling up the blankets and draping them around my shoulders. "And you're one of us, for the moment. I'll be right back. I need to find you a proper court gown, get some shoes on your feet."

"Shoes..." I wasn't sure I liked the idea.

"Yes, sunshine. You'll have to wear shoes."

"Even if I can't walk?"

"How long do you suppose it'll take you to learn to walk? Not long, I bet. You have good strong legs."

I clenched my knees together tight, as if I could will myself back to normal.

My tense form made him pause. He put his hands on my knees and gently moved them apart. A rush of heat swept over me, like I was back on the horse again. "Doesn't hurt, does it?" he asked.

"No..."

His eyes, blue-gray and beautiful, danced along my curves. I held my breath. I wondered if we had ever spoken of a moment like this, back when I was a mermaid. I wondered if we had ever talked about what it would be like, to be the same.

"Good," he said.

He left the room, shutting me in there alone. The room was huge, adorned with paintings and pieces of furniture made of a dark, solid wood. The only things within my reach from the bed were books, with writing on their surface. He had a few of them sitting on a little table next to where he slept.

I opened one and found a colored picture.

A picture? I had never realized books had pictures too. And this picture...it was a mermaid. A mermaid sitting on a rock and a man on the shore, reaching a hand out to clasp hers. The lines were so detailed that I was mesmerized. The mermaid and the man looked so yearning, but the shore was like a barrier between them, drawing a line they could never cross.

I slammed it shut. I didn't know how to feel.

I wondered if I was really here due to some sort of accident or chance...or if Wrindel had brought me here.

He had not been responsible for my loss of memory; no, I simply couldn't imagine that he would hurt me. Something didn't make sense, but it wasn't his fault. The way he looked at me...I knew he didn't want to hurt me. Quite the opposite.

I looked at my toes. I tried to move them and realized they could wiggle, each toe by itself.

I looked at the ceiling instead and took a long swig of ale.

Chapter Five

WRINDEL

GODS FORGIVE ME. Talwyn was in my bedroom and the fact of her existence was like a dream turned to reality. It was hitting me how badly I had always wanted her.

The image of her clamping those legs together was like a challenge. It was all new to her, even the sensations of having legs at all. I wanted to split her open. And by the look in her eyes, I don't think she'd complain when I did it.

A whole new world had opened up to us.

I took the stone from my pocket. I knew that damned witch had tricked me and every moment, I was falling into her trap. What was the trap? Simply to keep Talwyn with me forever? Maybe the witch and Talwyn had some sort of dispute.

Whatever it was, I couldn't ignore that the witch had granted Talwyn legs. She could take them away again.

Talwyn doesn't belong in the ocean. She belongs with me. It seemed I might lose my father too young, and I had never known my mother. For so many years, I'd been happy to amuse myself with courtesans and maids, women passing through town at the tavern, and the flirts of the court. Now my brother was getting married, and something inside me was changing, growing unsatisfied with fleeting pleasures.

I hurried up the stairs to a storage room containing dusty artifacts of kings past that were too important to give away and too ugly to pay attention to: everything from dull books, to gold-plated armor, to a clock that was particularly painful to look at, with no less than six naked cherubs. I opened a drawer to a chest with painted dragons that could only be described as foppish, and shoved the stone under some old papers. No one would ever look here. I don't when foppish dragons were in fashion, but not in my lifetime.

Guilt coursed through me. As if I was stuffing a piece of Talwyn's soul out of her sight.

Talwyn always told me she wanted to see more of this world. The look on her face when I brought her through the palace was worth more to me than gold. *Is it so terrible if I made Talwyn my bride? I'll have to prove to her that this place is worth leaving her old world behind.*

I told one of the maids to find Talwyn some clothes, and returned to her, locking and bolting the door behind me. Whatever older-and-wiser-brother lecture Ithrin wanted to give me, I didn't want to hear it.

When I opened the door, Talwyn was perched on the bed rummaging in my all my bedside drawers and drinking the ale. "I never knew books had so many pictures," she said. "But who is this?" She flashed a neatly framed pastel portrait of a lovely girl that she had found.

I frowned. "It isn't polite to poke in a man's drawers."

She laughed. "Oh no? I've heard that men like to have their drawers poked in."

"I mean—as much as I appreciate a good double entendre—" I took the picture from her, tossed it inside the top drawer, and slammed it shut with my fist. "I might keep private things in there."

"Private things? Like what?" She laughed as if it was a joke.

"You don't have any private things?"

"No. What do you mean...? Like hiding your valuables from thieves?" She seemed to realize this was not what troubled me. "In my world, it's very special to own rare things. Most things don't survive under the sea. When merfolk visit each other, the first thing they do is look around to see if their host owns anything rare. It's rude *not* to do that; it would indicate that I didn't think you had anything of value."

"Is that so? I suppose most things of a private nature *are* printed, so you wouldn't have them. Books, letters, diaries, pictures of loved ones... Now, *that* picture is of my favorite dancing girl in town."

Her brows briefly slammed downward with adorable chagrin. "Dancing girl?" she demanded.

I chuckled. "My late mother, actually." I edged closer to her and dared to slide a hand around her waist. She was still keeping her legs clamped together. "Have you no secrets at all, among the merfolk? No private possessions or places...no clothes, even..."

"No," she breathed.

I slid a hand up her thigh, bunching up her dress, slipping my fingers under the hem until I found the place where her legs met her sex. She had done nothing to stop me. My hand curved down until I found her slit, her lips smooth and already slick as could be. Her eyes widened. "You have a private place now, Talwyn."

"I feel different," she said. "I don't know if I like it." But then she shot me a furtive glance that said the opposite. "When we were riding...the horse..." Her breath came quick as I very gently stroked her there. "Wrin..."

"I know what you're trying to say. But don't tell me you don't like it, sunshine."

"A secret," she murmured. "It feels like having a place of my own—but you're the only one with the key."

"That's right. It is just for you and me. We can unlock things in each other that no one else can..." And even if I was far from being a virgin, that felt entirely true. Being with Talwyn was so different. "I've never wanted anyone like I want you now, Tal."

Chapter Six

TALWYN

I COULDN'T BREATHE. This was like nothing I had ever experienced before.

I was not myself. Having legs and clothes made everything different. In my world, sex was very straightforward. We had a season for mating, like animals do, although unlike animals, we had more self-control to resist the call and choose a mate for life. Despite my loss of memory, I felt sure I had never mated before. Our sexual organs stayed hidden behind an almost invisible slit of skin until the time came; I vaguely remembered a friend telling me "a man has a horn that comes out and goes into your cave", which was news to me at the time. Some humans thought we reproduced with our minds, or some strange magic, or that mermaids laid eggs.

I had heard mating was pleasurable. It was a fact of life no one was ashamed of. But I had gotten the sense that it was sort of like eating a nice meal. You did it, and it was enjoyable, and then it was done.

The pleasure I was feeling now was entirely different, as

Wrindel's hand forced its way into the hollow where my legs met my body, immediately finding that center point of incredible sensation. It had been stirred just a little before. But his fingers were blatant. I had no control over what I felt now; all the ale I'd consumed seemed to rush down there, a hot and unbidden feeling. His other hand was steady on my waist. The clothes I was wearing made it all seem secretive indeed; his hand shielded by the fabric so I didn't know quite what he was doing to me.

I kept my legs tight together, but it didn't matter; he could still fit his hand between them and get to such places that made me whimper.

"What is this?" I whispered as I felt something hot and wet spill out of me. For a second I was afraid I had peed on his hand. But it didn't actually feel like that at all. His fingers just felt even more slick as they rubbed against me.

"This is life on the surface, sunshine. What do you think?"

"I—I don't know."

"I won't hurt you. I told you I'd take care of you."

"It feels good. But my body is so different... I don't know if I like it."

"You want me to stop?"

I paused. "I do not."

He laughed. "I thought not. Sunshine, now that you have legs, I know exactly what to do with you. And I want to do *everything* to you...so badly. Even with legs, you're not like any other woman. You're my water spirit. I can smell the sea on your skin... in your hair... I want to show you every kind of pleasure."

I felt his steady hand on my rib cage against my heaving breaths. I shut my eyes. *This is not my world, not my body.* But I wanted to succumb so badly that I couldn't find the words to stop him. And I felt so comfortable with him, like he was the one person I could trust myself to be vulnerable around.

He pulled me onto his lap.

"It's okay to part your legs, sunshine. You know very well that you won't break." He tried to nudge me open wider but I did feel like I would break. He put his hands on my knees, his grip firm, and pushed the bony appendages apart until they bumped into the edge of the bed.

"Stay like that." His voice was commanding, but also soft. It instilled a sense of trust. "Let me see you." He pulled my dress up over my waist, and I lifted my arms to help him get it off my head. It was so strange and confining to wear clothes that I wasn't entirely sorry to be rid of them, even though it meant I could see my legs. His hands ran slowly up and down my thighs, his grip just firm enough to tell me that if I resisted, he would immediately push me open me again. I chewed my lip, hungry for something I couldn't quite define.

"You were always the girl I couldn't stop thinking about," he said. "Tail or legs. It doesn't matter. But...*this*." He slipped a finger within the slit between my legs again. "This is beautiful just for the promise of how many delights I can bring you."

"Is this...? I—I—" I stammered. I didn't know what to say.

He rubbed his fingers rapidly over the sensitive spot deep inside the folds, and what had been a delicious stimulation suddenly turned into sparks of almost agonizing desire. "Wrindel...oh—oh, what are you doing to me?"

"Talwyn..." He suddenly pressed his mouth to mine, and I opened my lips readily. His fingers drew away from my center, leaving warmth behind—but also emptiness. I practically sucked his tongue into my mouth, wanting more of him. I heard the intimate, soft sound of his breath drawing in sharply, close to my ears. I had never experienced sound like this, either. Underwater, sounds were soft and wavy and traveled differently. On the shore, everything was drowned by the sound of the roaring water.

This was so quiet. I could hear every rustle, every little catch in his breath—and my own. His hand in my hair, the brush of strands against skin. The rougher texture of his clothes as I plucked at his collar, the sound of his hand sliding on my smooth skin.

"You're so sleek," he said, his voice rough with lust. "I want to show you my world, Talwyn. Gods, I want to make you happy. I want to spread your lovely legs until you can hardly bear how wide I've split you open, and then I want to spear you deep."

"It—it sounds painful," I said, but I felt that strange hot wetness rush out of me.

"Do you think I want to cause you anything but pleasure right now?"

"N—no."

"The only pain I want to bring you is very sweet. If you don't enjoy it, you can tell me to stop. Is it better if you can't see your legs?"

"Maybe."

He swept a hand around my waist and deftly flipped me onto my stomach. His bed was so soft, it was almost like floating. He climbed over me and his fingers traveled down my stomach. He found that sensitive place again, his hand teasing and caressing, but now I really couldn't see him or anything he was doing.

His knees planted on the inside of mine. I felt his legs, large and muscular compared to mine. Now he pushed his legs outward, forcing my knees apart on the outside of his, spreading me open against all my instincts. Just as he promised, my muscles were strained almost to the point of pain—but stopped short of that. My hands were spread out on the covers, my head pressed into his pillows. I felt his rigid manhood pent by his trousers, but resting against my ass. Now both of his hands reached around my front and gently pulled the folds wide apart.

"Better now?" he asked again.

I was trying to gather my thoughts, and I couldn't. I could only moan. He was overwhelming me. "Wrindel..."

One single fingertip firmly flicked across the bud that was now as exposed as could be. Once, twice...again and again.

I screamed, my hips bucking as I tried to flee the intensity of the sensation. That finger was unrelenting. My legs couldn't close. Two of the fingers on his left hand kept me spread wide while that other finger, large and rough the way the hands of surface dwelling men always were, just kept stroking and stroking. And then a second joined in. Now they both stroked faster as I rode waves of sweet torture like nothing I'd ever felt. Soon I felt like he could have done anything to me and I wouldn't have cared, just as long as this feeling broke before it killed me.

I was split like a shell and my skin was burning, especially where he touched me. His warm body was comforting even as his finger gave me the most agonizing pleasure. Slow pulses shot down to my core, and then they came faster and faster.

Suddenly my whole body rushed toward a finale, and my scream pitched higher like I was underwater. I couldn't help it. I had lost all control as my body throbbed against his touch. His touch gentled as my screams died to whimpers. I drifted back to earth slowly.

I shuddered, limp against the pillow.

He sat up and flopped beside me instead, pulling me against him, smoothing my hair. "Talwyn...gods, that was lovely, and that was just the beginning of what I can do to you."

I felt very tender in that secret place, but also strangely unsatisfied. His hand caressed me, down my arm and the planes of my stomach. His fingers rubbed my inner thigh, as if reminding me that I was not a mermaid anymore, that I had been transformed into something else, something that felt as if it belonged to him.

I'm not sure I had ever felt so peaceful, so present in the moment.

"I didn't realize how nice it was to have things...done to me," I murmured.

Someone banged on the door.

"Not now," he called.

"Your highness, I beg your pardon—I have a dress I believe will fit the lady?"

"Damn it, all right. Wait here," he said, as if I would do anything else.

Chapter Seven

WRINDEL

I OPENED the door to take the dress—and a larger hand than I expected shoved it open. The maid was standing there looking nervous, while my brother peered past me and got a good look at Talwyn's naked body. Then he grabbed my arm. "I want to talk to you—*now*."

I stepped out, shoving him off, straightening my shirt. "Whatever you want to lecture me about, it's not your business."

Ithrin lifted up a book called "Enchantments of the Sea". It was never good news when anyone carried a book around just to prove a point. I shut the door on Talwyn, giving my brother an impatient look while he said, "You just stole a mermaid bride. Didn't you?"

"She's not my bride."

"If she's just your dalliance, that might be even worse. What did you steal from her? You need to give it back."

"Calm down. What does this book of yours have to say? It looks like it's about two hundred years old, for starters."

"It is...let's see..." He opened it to the frontispiece and said imperiously, "Eighty-two years old."

I shrugged.

"'Many men are lured by these beautiful creatures, despite their fish tails,'" he read.

"Fish tails? Not exactly," I said. "Mermaids are mammals."

"Mm-*hmm*," Ithrin said, with an annoying lift of his brows. He continued, "'It is possible to make a bride of them. Some merfolk carry an enchanted talisman such as a necklace or comb made from a shore-stone. If a man steals the talisman, the mermaid will become his forever, with her tail split into legs. If you manage to capture one of these rare creatures and wish to keep her, you must never return the talisman to her. She will snatch it up in a moment and return to the sea.' Sound familiar? You said a witch had a hand in this..."

"I just wanted to protect her. I had little choice."

"You stole her," Ithrin said. "You have to give the talisman back so she can go home."

"It's not that simple. The witch *wanted* me to steal her. If I send her back to the sea, she might be in danger, and by then the magic is broken and I wouldn't be able to protect her even if I needed to. It would be too late. I can't send her back to the sea unless I know she's safe there."

"And what if you find out she is safe?" Ithrin asked. "What then? Will you send her home?"

"Of course," I said, but admittedly without conviction. "Unless she wants to stay. And then I'd move mountains to let her stay." I knocked the side of one fist into the unyielding stone wall. "I've been getting to know to that girl for months now," I said.

"Months? I thought you just met the other day."

"No. When I walk on the beach sometimes, I often see her there."

"Why didn't you mention her earlier?"

I rubbed my head. "I don't know. I think it's because I liked her more than I wanted to admit. It was easier not to tell anyone. But we talked a lot. She travels around, picking things from shipwrecks. She's seen interesting things; shipwrecked galleons with chest of gold still locked inside and old, old long-ships from the Northland raiders. She asked me a lot of questions about my life, too. It was just...very enjoyable."

"Yes," Ithrin said icily. "You could try talking to women on land a little more before you try to get under their skirts."

I shoved the book back at him. "I don't always *like* who I am. I don't need you to remind me. At least I wasn't talking to the dead. That could've gotten you killed."

"And I'm done with that now."

"I'm trying to move on, too. But I want to move on with *her*."

"And yet I see that you've moved past the talking already, now that she's got the right parts. You're back to your old ways the second you're presented with the opportunity."

"Ithrin—get out of my business," I said. "I know what I'm doing."

"No, you don't." He jabbed a finger toward the door. "You're risking her happiness. If it's true that you really know the person she can't remember being, and you have feelings for her, you can't just resort to the same old tricks, or it's going to be a relationship as pointlessly superficial as all the rest."

"Like you're an expert now. I know far more about relationships with women than you do."

"And don't tell Father about this. You know he won't want you getting involved with a mermaid."

He foisted the book onto me before walking away.

"Like he's not going to find out!" I barked, and then I sobered. Maybe he wouldn't, confined to his bed.

I'd always told myself I knew far more about women than Ithrin, because I was experienced while he waited for his future wife. Now that Ithrin had a wife, he thought he knew better. And maybe he did. Ithrin was taking life seriously. His relationship was real, and my life seemed a game in comparison.

I thought about Ithrin and Ellara, how he was teaching her to ride, how they took walks and fed the ducks in the moat and sat there talking. I'd never had that with anyone—except Talwyn.

And no way in hell could I keep my courtship with Talwyn

chaste now that she was here. It didn't negate all of our conversations. The time we had spent made the sex that much better. She might not remember the time we'd spent but...deep down, I thought she knew.

I opened the door. She was still there naked in my bed, just where I left her.

"Talwyn," I said, sitting down beside her.

"Wrindel..." She glanced at me, her eyes slightly glazed before they focused on mine.

"Let's get some clothes on you."

"What were you yelling about out there?"

"Nothing of concern." I picked up one of her feet and rolled a peach-colored silk stocking up one perfectly shaped leg. She squirmed a little; I could tell she didn't really like having her legs encased in fabric. It must've felt very strange to her.

"I heard some of it," she said, arching a brow.

"Great."

"Why don't you like who you are?"

"It's not that. Don't take things out of context."

"You sleep with a lot of women, don't you?" she said, her tone almost sly. It suggested she wasn't going to hate me for it, but she was definitely going to hassle me.

"Not now," I said sharply. "It's only you, sunshine—as long as I can keep you. But I also need to get married."

"Oh?"

"If my father dies—" I fastened a garter belt around her waist and clipped the stockings to it. Many elven women only wore a simple shift for underwear and put their bare feet into slippers, but I preferred having a few things to strip off. The maid who brought me the clothes must have heard rumors of my proclivities. I paused a moment at the sight of her gorgeous little pussy between all those trappings. Such smooth bare skin she had. Even girls who put wax down there to tear out their hair didn't look like that. "You're so beautiful..."

She wasn't having it now. "If your father dies, what?"

"Ithrin is the king. I'm the second in line until Ellara has a child. And if something happened to Ithrin, I would be prince regent until his son came of age. I would expect Ithrin to live a long life, but our family hasn't had the best of luck. I know everyone in Wyndyr would feel more secure if we both settled down."

"Why haven't you settled down already? You don't like any elven girls?"

"I like a lot of elven girls. But—" I clasped her hand. "Not as much as you."

"You're a sweet talker, aren't you?"

"But I mean it. I want you, and no one else. As I said, we've known each other for six months. This is no hasty declaration."

She paused, slowly tilting her head sideways, so her long, untamed hair fell across one shoulder. "Are you...proposing to me?"

I hadn't intended to propose to her, but I realized that not only was I doing exactly that. For months I had wanted her, closing my mind off to the prospect only because I could never have her. Now—now I *must* have her.

Gods, could I only have her if I kept up the lie? If I never told her about the stone? If I never told her she had two sisters who would no doubt be worried sick? They were of age, although just barely, and she seemed a little frustrated with them when we talked, but was that justification for stealing her away from them?

But if the other choice was to put her in danger...

The witch was forcing me to choose Talwyn's course in life. I couldn't ask her what she wanted. If I returned her to the sea, she would know I was an honest man, but I could never get her back.

Was I wrong to keep her here? Maybe fate had brought her to me.

"Why postpone the inevitable?" I said. "Some things must happen. The sun rises, the sun sets, and I have to ask you to marry me."

Chapter Eight

Talwyn

Objectively, this seemed like such a bad idea.

But I think he had bewitched me.

"I need my memories," I said. "Before I can decide."

His hand tightened around my palm. "What if you could only get your memory back by returning to the sea forever? What would you choose?"

"Is that how it is?"

"Maybe... I don't really know how or why you're here any more than you do..." He was hesitant. "I have a feeling your memories are the key to finding out how I came to find you on the shore. But this might be the price you pay for being here. That's all I can say."

"I don't know, Wrin... What if I have family I've left behind? Did I ever mention it?"

"No." His pose had grown stiff. "We didn't talk about our families."

"What did we talk about?"

"Hopes and dreams." He smiled faintly. "Gossip. The

weather. Food. Judge me if you will—and you did—but I still think the humble cod is the tastiest fish."

"Not enough fat in cod." I frowned. "You're trying to change the subject."

He finally got to his feet and sat down on the bed beside me. "You kept my mind off of things, sunshine. I wish you remembered our conversations. But since you don't, we can talk it out all over again. Let me show you everything palace life has to offer, and then you can decide whether your answer is yes or no."

"All right," I said, unable to ignore the excitement quivering inside me, much less an unbidden curiosity to know what else he might do to me.

"First, court dress," he said, holding the neck over my head. I was starting to understand how clothes worked a little better. I lifted my arms and let him slip the dress on. At least this dress was more comfortable than the other one. The fabric was very thin and soft, almost as silky against my skin as water itself. It had loose, fluttering sleeves, a low neckline and a high waist.

"Second, let's get you on your feet." He tugged on my hands.

"Ack!" He pulled me up so I was standing on shaky legs, leaning heavily on his grasp.

"You're no infant with undeveloped muscles," he said. "So you should be able to walk, I think."

"But I don't know how to balance on these tiny feet!"

"They're not much tinier than mine, by the looks of it."

"Are you saying my feet are too big?"

"Nothing wrong with it. But you're not a small girl. You're almost as tall as I am."

Truly, he still had a good several inches on me, but I guess he was tall for a man, and I was tall for a woman. It was strange to consider because mermaids didn't measure things in terms of height, only length. But in my world, anyone could move in any direction, whereas I realized here, feet were rooted to the ground.

"Take a minute to find your center," he said.

My hips wavered, trying to find any such thing. "It's so

different under water, Wrin! I don't know how to stand up rigidly like you do."

He put a hand at the small of my back, and straightened me up, stepping close to me so that my stomach rested against his pelvis. Having him that close offered an extra sense of security. His hands moved to my hips, keeping me secure. I shuffled my feet a little so that my stance fit better with the way he was holding me. And somehow, I found myself standing straight, albeit with little muscles in my legs trembling.

"That's it," he said. "Do you feel secure now?"

"Not exactly... Don't let go of me!"

"We'll go slowly." He moved his hands away from my hips, up to my arms, and held me as I quivered, trying to find the right way of standing on my own.

"There's no guidebook for this," he commented wryly. "I know how to teach a baby to walk. The healers have helped men who were injured build up their strength again. But a girl with two strong, healthy legs who just doesn't know how to use them? It ought to be easy."

"So *you* say."

But I realized I was standing up straight again, and he had been slowly loosening his grip on me a bit.

We kept working on it until I dared to attempt a few steps forward, falling into his arms. He caught me and broke into a wide smile that matched my own.

"I did it!" I said, caught in a moment of ridiculous triumph.

"Baby's first steps," he teased.

"Now—can any of the other women you've been with do *that*?" I poked his ribs.

His grin shifted into something that reminded me of the words I'd overheard—*I don't always like who I am*. "That's the third thing, sunshine. Ithrin already warned you about me. Everyone will warn you about me. And if you had your memories, you would already know. It's true—I've made no secret of it. I've been chasing girls since I was sixteen, and I'm a prince, so I catch about every one. I've been losing my taste for the endless pursuit, seeing Ithrin and Ellara so happy together. But I can't blame you if you look at my reputation and you don't believe me. I know mermen aren't as subject to that kind of behavior."

"I don't know. I feel as if I've heard stories."

"I thought merfolk have a mating season."

"Well, yes, but how much can *you* get done in a season? And it's—well—it comes around about every other month for ten or twelve days. Not all merfolk are sweet, simple village types, you know. But I've stayed away from mermen."

"Why's that?"

"I guess I just...didn't feel anything for them. Or maybe I had something else I had to do..."

He seemed eager to change the subject now. "Anyway, it's time we should head to the dining hall. I suppose I can carry you...this once."

"You'd better."

He swept me into his arms. "Luckily, we are not *too* formal around here," he said.

I gasped as we entered the dining hall. A long table was set with piles of bread, silver tureens with three different soups, and most astonishing of all, three candelabras with a dozen candles each. The candles caught the light of silver and glass and made everything so bright that I could clearly see the faces of every person at the table. Off to one side was a small fountain where diners could rinse and dry their hands. Rose petals floated in the basin, which was tiled in a mosaic pattern.

Wrindel put me on my feet so we could wash our hands together. Everyone was looking at us, but I couldn't feel too embarrassed—not yet. It was too dreamlike. Why be embarrassed inside of a dream?

"Everything here is so...deliberate," I said.

"Deliberate?"

"I mean, all the little details." I rinsed my hands, noticing that the pattern of tiles at the bottom of the basin was like an octopus reaching its arms up the sides. The water felt wonderful on my skin. "The merfolk are like animals in comparison. Living in caves. We have no cuisine, no...houses made to look so nice?"

"Architecture?"

"Is that what you call it?"

He nodded. "I'm not showing you all of this to make you feel inferior about your home," he said. "The underwater world must be beautiful." He handed me a linen towel to dry my hands.

"It is, but...we are not masters of our world, the way land people are."

"Masters of our world, are we? In some ways." He touched my arm. "Let's get you seated." He swept me off my feet again, prompting a squeak of surprise from me and gentle laughter from the girl sitting beside Prince Ithrin. I was given a seat across from her.

"This is Ellara," Ithrin said. "My bride."

"Nice to meet you." Ellara readily offered a hand across the table, then glanced at Ithrin. "I'm not supposed to reach across, am I?" We shook hands anyway. "I'm still learning the palace etiquette sometimes," she said.

"Well, we aren't sticklers," Ithrin said. "But a princess needs to know how to be a stickler if she must."

"Good thing I'm not a princess," I murmured, looking at the array of silverware. I had some idea of how they worked, but why I had three forks was beyond me.

Beside the brothers, the head of the table was empty, a sad reminder that the king was sick. But we were hardly alone at the long table. There were a good twenty or so more finely clad ladies and gentlemen seated at the long table, speaking amongst themselves—probably about me, although I couldn't quite make

"Who are all of those people?" I asked Wrindel.

"The highest ranked members of the court besides us," he said. "That's Lord Pirell, Lady Pirell, across from them is Lord and Lady Moridan...you know what, it doesn't really matter right now."

Next to the Lord and Lady Pirell was a skinny blonde girl who was glaring at me. I ignored her in favor of Ellara, who seemed friendly. She was petite and darker than the elves, with coarser hair that curled wildly, barely tamed by a pearl headband. Her eyes were bright and golden, and seemed like they wouldn't miss a thing.

"You're a mermaid," Ellara said. "All of this must seem very strange. Have you ever been on land before?"

"No...it's all new to me. And you're...a goblin?"

"Half goblin, but...well, that counts for a full goblin around these parts." Her nose scrunched.

"Has anyone been unkind to you lately?" Ithrin asked with concern.

"No, no, they're very polite, it's just—not entirely welcoming. But you know, I'm used to that. I can handle it." She added, "We're going to the goblin kingdom in the spring and I'm very excited for *him* to be the one out of his element for once. Just to be fair."

"But *there*, you'll be half-elf, won't you?" Wrindel teased. He passed me some food and showed me how to spread the butter on the bread. I almost hated to hack into the butter because it was so pretty, formed in a molded shape like a running horse.

I cut the horse's tail off and tried to spread it on my bread. I was clumsy with the silverware. I noticed the other diners whispering down from one end of the table toward us in a chain of hands cupped around ears, and Lord Pirell cleared his throat and said, "Does your dear father know you have caught a mermaid?"

Ithrin glanced at Wrindel, who looked back at him defiantly. "No," Wrindel said. "And you won't tell him, either."

"You *do* know that—"

"If you're referring to the events of two centuries ago, yes, I know. And it is hardly relevant."

"Two centuries ago?" I asked.

"When grandfather was young, he brought a mermaid to the palace," Ithrin said. "People said she was his mistress, but she didn't have legs. I'm sure they never...copulated. She lived in the palace waters for many months."

"Does that mean I'm a scandal?" I asked.

That blonde girl was giving me a cold look, but when she caught me looking at her, she took out a compact with a jeweled case and pretended to straighten the gold combs in her hair.

"Of course not. The royal family have the power to make

their own decisions," Lord Pirell said, but he looked at Wrindel like a judgmental uncle.

"Is a mermaid worse than a goblin?" Ellara whispered.

"We're not about to start ranking the races of the world based on how appropriate they are," Ithrin said uncomfortably. "This is a modern era. We should all be working together."

But I'm not sure it was really that simple. The dinner was the best thing I'd ever tasted—fish baked with herbs and lemon, roasted squash, beans mashed with onion and dark sugar, tiny carrots swimming in butter—but I was so awkward with the utensils that I sent one of the carrots flying to the floor. I got lemon sauce on my dress, too. I wasn't used to eating like this, with clothes to worry over, and objects that fell instead of floating, and no water to wash everything away. When I joined humans on the beach in a festival atmosphere, everyone was half-drunk so it didn't matter.

I felt a little ashamed of myself, like I was a slob with bad manners, but in my underwater world I knew how to behave. My world was so different from theirs, not just in culture but even on a basic elemental level. I suppose they couldn't help but be suspicious of me.

It only made me more stubborn. I wasn't sure I had ever felt like I belonged, even back home. But when I was with Wrindel, I felt like someone was listening to me. I didn't want to give that up, not just because some snooty elves didn't like mermaids.

After dinner, the crowd retired to a series of salons on the ground floor of the palace. The party swelled, joined by many who had not been present in the dinner hall. Older gentlemen took to one room and older ladies to another, while the younger folk mixed, playing games with dice. I didn't know what dice were called right up until then, but I recognized them from shipwrecks.

"I'm so glad to know what these are actually for!" I told Wrindel.

"The question now is, how good are you at tossing them?"

Pretty good, as it turned out. We had eight people at our table and I won the first two games out of six.

"Beginner's luck, fishy," the blonde girl said sourly as I swept up the chips. She had been increasingly nasty to me, and the rest of the time she spent more time staring at her compact. I'm not sure what was so interesting about her own face.

"It's not just luck," I retorted. "There's a trick to deciding how many dice to use and when." I was feeling pretty pleased at myself for realizing this early on.

All the guys at the table said a collective, "Oooh", like they thought we were going to fight.

"It's *mostly* luck," the girl said. "Kind of like fucking a prince these days. Goblins and mermaids? What next?" She looked at Wrindel and slammed her dice down.

"Oh, Wrindel, you never should've dallied with that one," one of the boys said, a red-headed elf who had been drinking a lot.

Wrindel's fair, lovely elven skin flushed so easily that he couldn't hide any embarrassment. He took a swig of wine and told me, "Gods, I'm sorry. I told you I have a history."

"With *that* girl?"

"With every girl," said the oh-so-helpful redhead.

"You stay out of it," Wrindel snapped at him. "Not every girl."

Ithrin glanced over from another table playing a sedate card game. My eyes followed the blonde girl. She had walked over to another table to talk to a different girl, and they were both shooting nasty looks our way.

"Wrindel," I hissed. "How many girls here thought *they* might be your bride?"

"I never promised anything to any of them," he said. "It isn't my fault if they make presumptions."

"And how many girls in this room have you slept with?"

"None."

"None?"

"My favorite chambermaid moved on."

"Don't joke with me." I put down the dice. "If I'm even to consider marrying you for two seconds, I need complete honesty from you."

"I am being honest," he said. "I don't sleep with ladies of the court. I stick to proper courtesans who know what they're doing, most of the time. I don't want any bastards."

"Oh," I said, not pleased at this thought either. "Then why are these women acting like this?"

"I have done a few...*other* things with—Kiara—and Meriam, over there..."

For a moment I was furious with him, hot with jealousy. Yes, he'd warned me. That hardly mattered.

"I'm not going to apologize for things I've done before I ever met you," he said.

The blonde girl put down her compact like she had just decided something, while her friend flapped her hands like she wanted to stop her. She walked back over to us. "The king is ill," she said. "You know the old story about King Lefior. The poor mermaid lurking in the palace. The shame. Don't you owe your people a proper bride?"

"You're jealous, Kiara," he said. "We have always courted for love in this kingdom as often as not."

"I'm not jealous; I don't want you. Definitely not now."

"Watch yourself," he said. "You forget that I am your prince."

"Oooh, are you going to throw me in a dungeon for talking back?" Her friend tried to pull her back to their table as another man joined the argument, taking her side more diplomatically.

"Wrin, you have to admit, you weren't very fair to Kiara," he said.

Wrin stood. "Fair? I never made promises to anyone. Nor did I offer anything you weren't *eager* to receive," he told her, his tone dangerous.

"You cad," she said.

I took a stumbling step back from the table.

Maybe I've made a terrible mistake. Could I really trust Wrindel? Maybe I felt so comfortable with him because he was charming any time he wished to be.

If I did decide to stay with him, I refused to be seen as a poor mermaid lurking in the palace, a girl who couldn't walk or read or use a fork.

I rested my eyes on Kiara's compact, abandoned on the table

as everyone's attention was drawing into a circle of accusations. I slipped out of my chair and crawled toward the other table. Ithrin was trying to calm everyone down, only drawing fire of his own for choosing a goblin girl over an elf. "Half-elf!" he insisted.

I snatched the compact off the table and shoved it between my breasts. Then I made my way to the door, clutching at furniture to keep my balance. Various small muscles I'm not sure I had until today were quivering in protest. I could stand up as long as I clung to the wall, but I was afraid to walk without support. I really just wanted to go back to the bedroom.

A moment later, Ellara stepped out and found me hesitating. "Are you all right?" she asked.

"Oh, I'm fine," I said.

"High elves are a lot more petty than I thought they'd be," she said. "I had an idea that they were always sophisticated, like the way I remember my father. Turns out, if you live to be two hundred plus, you really nurse old family wounds. Not so different from goblins, in the end!"

"Who was this mermaid mistress everyone's whispering about?"

"I don't know. But hey, maybe we could find out. I would imagine that all the papers of the old kings and queens are in the library's archives."

"I would need your help," I admitted. "I can't read."

"No shame in that. Lots of people can't," Ellara said. "Of course I'd help. Selfishly, I hope you'll stay. I can already tell that everyone would talk about me a lot less if you were here." She noticed how I clung to the wall. "Do you need help getting somewhere?"

"It's been a long night. I'd like to just go to bed. But I can't walk either," I said. "I'm not sure you're big enough to help me."

"I'm stronger than I look!" Ellara said. "Let's see." She slung my arm around her shoulders and put a hand around my waist. My balance was improving, and I managed to walk away from the wall, leaning on her when I tottered.

"Ohh, it's a long way back to the bedroom," I said.

"Don't think of it like that. Just one step at a time, and you're getting better."

"Do you think I can trust Wrindel to have truly changed his ways?" I asked her.

"I'll tell you what I know about these brothers," she said. "They've grown up under a load of grief after the death of their mother and two eldest siblings. Ithrin was a little boy, and Wrindel was a baby. So Wrin never knew the lost half of the family, and he was learning to walk and talk as his father and brother were just trying to put themselves back together. I can only imagine how awful it was for everyone. From what I understand, the king and queen were a true love match." She paused. "Sometimes I don't understand why the world has to be so sad."

The story pricked at my memories. As if I knew a little of how this felt.

"Wrindel might have a bad reputation with women," Ellara continued. "But one thing I've learned about him is that he takes care of everyone. He doesn't like to see anyone hurting. If something troubles you, you hardly have to say anything—he'll make you laugh or hand you a warm drink. I've seen how he balances out Ithrin, who is more serious. Maybe he was just searching for love, like we all are. Or maybe he didn't want to be seen as too much of a caretaker. A prince needs to have manly prowess, you know. But then again, maybe he just has a hell of a libido. Ithrin's like a sleeping dragon." She grinned. "Don't tell him I said that."

"If that's all it is..."

"You think you can handle him?"

"Oh, I think I could." If it meant he was going to do things like he'd already done to me, over and over... I flushed.

Ellara giggled. "They are pretty, pretty men, aren't they?"

Chapter Nine

Wrindel

"She can't even use a fork correctly!" Kiara cried. "If I see her at dinner again, I'll tell my father to tell the king." She had reached the point where she knew she had lost the general argument—she couldn't tell me what to do—but refused to give up.

"Enough." Ithrin stood next to me, his voice slicing through the chatter. "You will not tell the king. That's my call. He's not well right now, and I don't want anything to upset him. Whatever your personal judgment might be on Wrindel's choices, he is well within his rights."

I glanced at Ithrin, thankful that he had kept his own concerns out of the public sphere. I knew he wasn't happy about this either, but he was a loyal brother.

Somehow, I realized, I had lost track of Talwyn in the middle of our heated argument. "Where's Talwyn?" I hissed at him, as the disgruntled young nobles settled back into their games.

"Ellara's gone too. They're probably together. I wouldn't worry. Play a game of Demon's Hand with me and then see if she's in bed." He picked up a deck and neatly shuffled it. "Of course, you *should* offer her a guest room."

I shrugged noncommittally.

"You've asked for this, you know," Ithrin said. "Girls don't seem to mind as much when you're known to flirt with everyone. But choosing a mermaid, ignoring all the elven girls, without even holding a ball?"

"Yes. I get the picture. *Everyone* has made it very clear to me by now. Let's talk about something else."

Ithrin dealt me a hand. "I believe that you genuinely have feelings for her. You've never been so stubborn about it before. But you also have a tendency not to take consequences seriously. You stole that girl from the sea. You stole her memories."

"I'm going to take her to the healers to see about her memories."

"The healers can't do anything for her! You bloody well know that already. Her memories are gone because you're holding her talisman, isn't that right?"

"You read that in an old book; we can't be sure."

Ithrin snorted.

Unreasonable anger bubbled inside me. He wasn't telling me anything I didn't know. I had fallen into a trap, as easily as a mouse: lie to Talwyn, or lose her. I discarded my two of clubs and drew a new card. I won the game, but I barely said another word to Ithrin.

When I came back to my room, Talwyn was sleeping, curled up on the fur in front of the fireplace. Her dress was tossed across the bed, but she was still wearing the stockings and garters. *Gods.*

Clearly, she wasn't angry at me despite the scene earlier.

"Tal?" I whispered.

She really was asleep. I took off my boots, and then my shirt, but as I pulled the clothing over my head, I noticed something on my nightstand.

Kiara's jeweled compact.

Talwyn had stolen it? I didn't know whether to laugh or groan.

I settled myself behind her and draped an arm over her. She stirred, shifting onto her back.

"Why aren't you in bed?" I asked.

"I'm having a hard time getting used to all the clothes and coverings...but I was cold, too. It's nice here by the fire."

"But you left the stockings on."

"I had some idea that you wanted to take them off..."

"You liked it earlier, didn't you?"

She gave me an impish smile. "I think I need more of it before I can decide for sure."

I leaned to kiss her, and she crashed her lips into mine first. I slipped my tongue into her mouth and she opened wide for me. That mouth of hers was going to be good for a lot of things. Despite the meal, she still tasted like the sea, clean and a little salty. I pumped my tongue in and out of her mouth, deeply, and she responded in kind. Her knees were locked together again, and I forced them open. She made a little sound in my mouth like it hurt. I loved how just spreading her legs felt like I was doing something really intense.

But before this got too hot, I remembered the compact. "Why did you steal that thing?"

"Because..." Talwyn paused like deep down, she wasn't entirely sure why. "I'll give it back."

"That's no answer."

"I think I just wanted to show you," she said.

"Show me? Don't you mean you wanted to show her?"

"Well, both of you," she said. "I've always been independent and if I give that up, it won't be to take crap from any girl who has a history with you. I'm not sure how ladies are supposed to act around here, but I have my pride. Your history ends with me."

"I accept those terms." I kissed her again. Her bold words only heightened my lust, made me want to drive her harder because I knew she could take it. Talwyn never talked to me like I was royalty. Our lips grew more urgent. She stroked my hair, her hands open wide so that her fingers raked across my whole scalp at once. We rolled around on the fur. I stroked my erection against her clit through my trousers.

"I want you," I said.

"I want you too." She sucked in a ragged breath. "Even if you are a cad."

Chapter Ten

TALWYN

I REACHED DOWN and tried to unbutton his clothes. I knew what buttons were, and they seemed pretty easy to manage, but right now I was having trouble.

He unfastened them for me. I dragged them off his legs. He was fair, athletically built—exquisite. Legs might be strange, but they were also fascinating. I ran my hands along his thighs and up to his buttocks, feeling his skin tense and shiver with desire wherever my hands graced his flesh. His cock stood, stiff and thicker than I imagined. I touched it hesitantly.

He half-smiled. "You won't hurt me, sunshine. Might as well get to know what's about to split you open."

I don't know why such talk made my body so eager, like his manhood was a meal I'd already sampled, and I knew just how good it would taste. "Seriously, now...will it hurt?"

"It usually does. But not the way other things hurt." He brushed my hair away from my neck, the gesture so tender. "I'll make you ready for me. You'll be begging, Tal, I promise."

He dropped kisses down my neck all the way to my breasts.

His mouth drew in my nipple, nibbling all around the tight skin, and instantly I knew what he meant. Somehow, I could feel what he was doing all the way down between my legs. I moaned as he nibbled and suckled, first one and then the other. I kicked my feet, finally digging them into the fur to stop myself.

He took one of my hands and put it between my legs. I stiffened. I had never felt down there myself, and it was strange. The skin was so velvety, and so slick.

"Feel how wet you are," he said.

"I—I must be making a mess of your rug."

"Not yet. But it's kind of an old rug anyway. It was some poor thing my uncle shot." He guided my fingers to the swollen, tender bud. "That's your clit, sunshine. They don't get as much attention in the popular consciousness as they should, but your clit perks up as sure as a cock when its paid its due." He pushed my fingers along the slick folds. "And down here is where I'll enter you. It's wet because it knows. And I say this with complete honesty—you have the sexiest damn pussy I've ever seen."

I was blushing furiously. "That can't be true."

"You're so soft and bare. Not a thing to get in my way when I taste you. Women of the land have hair there. Mind you, some men don't like a woman to shave bare. It can make you look more childlike and I do like a woman to be a *woman*. But with you, there is no mistaking that. Your curves, sunshine...they'll be dancing in my head until the day I die, no matter what happens."

He started kissing down my stomach now, down one of my hips. He pushed my legs open again—I had hardly been conscious of closing them, but it was second nature to me for my body to move like I still had a tail—and I moaned weakly.

His tongue slid along my sensitive clit in a slow rhythm. I whimpered, arching my hips toward him, wanting more and more.

"Oh, Wrin...can you go harder?"

"No," he said. "When I'm inside you, then you can ask that question."

It was true. The longer his tongue glided along my slick skin, the more I craved him inside me. Needed him like nothing else.

He slipped a finger just inside my entrance, and then he traced the wet finger around my back passage, just barely nudging at my asshole. I tensed with surprise.

"Don't worry," he said. "That's something for later. But it never hurts to tease."

I was shocked that when he drew his finger away, I missed the touch. "What happens there?"

"I can fuck you there too," he said. "I know you're about to protest the idea. But you're intrigued. You're even wetter and pinker than before."

I *was* about to protest the idea, but I remembered Ellara telling me that Wrindel took care of other people. In this moment, I could feel how much he wanted me to be happy. Whatever he wanted to do to me, I could feel that it wasn't just a selfish act. He wanted us to be close in every way. If what Ellara said was true about Wrindel never even knowing half of his family, it made perfect sense that he would crave connection.

In the end, I'm not sure why I trusted him so much. Why I was willing to surrender these most sacred parts of myself to him. Logically, maybe I shouldn't. But something that went far past logic surged through me when I was with him.

The merfolk said the sea asks you not to think, but just to be. I could never get there under the waters. I had never gotten there until now, in his arms.

"You're ready, aren't you?" he asked. "More than ready."

"Oh, yes. I—" I looked at his cock again and it seemed even stiffer than before, with a bead of moisture on the tip. "I—I think so."

"How about this, sunshine? I think you like to have a little control over your world. I'll sit on the bed and you can sit on *me*."

He was right about that. I didn't want to surrender to him completely until I understood what I was getting into.

He carried me to the edge of the bed and sat down, guiding me onto his lap facing him, urging me to put my knees on the bed and straddle him. He was a pretty broad figure to straddle. I clutched his shoulders, gnawing at my lip as I let my legs adjust to this sensation.

"That's it. Spread as wide as you can." He stroked my thighs, encouraging me. My skin tingled. I lowered my body toward his shaft, finding the head.

"Relax your muscles," he said. "It's going to feel so wonderful to join with you, Tal."

I knew I had the right position, so there was nothing to do now but let it happen. I lowered myself onto his cock, groaning at the pain I knew would come. It was like spreading my legs magnified by a hundred—a splitting violation that felt like I was tearing in two, but at the same time, it was a delicious feeling. Loving someone. Trusting someone. Giving myself over to something larger than myself.

It was also sweet. So very sweet. I felt so tight and the way he filled me up, stretched me deep inside...I was surprised at just how right it felt.

"You might not be able to take the whole thing on the first try," he said.

"Is that a challenge?"

"If you want to make it into one..."

"I want to be the best you've ever had, Prince Wrindel," I said, shoving his hair out of his eyes and kissing him deeply as I kept pushing myself to have every inch of him inside me. I made mingled sounds of pain and pleasure, my mouth drinking him in. I felt every small increment like it was a great accomplishment, his hard length reaching deeper as I rocked my hips slowly, finding the room for him. It got easier, as I kept getting more and more slick inside.

His hips flexed, his cock throbbing inside me. "That's all of me," he said. Slowly, he started to take control. He rolled his hips, clutching my ass, his cock stroking me inside, his pelvis rubbing gently against my clit. "Oh, Tal, I've wanted this. Now I don't know how I held back all summer from even kissing you. But I'm glad we waited. I never realized how satisfying it is to wait."

"I think I've wanted this all summer too," I said. "I think I was afraid of how much I was starting to like you. I wish I could remember all the things we've talked about."

He pulled me down on top of him, our limbs so tangled that I felt like we were two halves of the same octopus. He swept me under him, pumping into me faster. He looked strangely serious in the moment. He looked at me like he was memorizing every line of my face.

He worries he might lose me, I thought.

Right now, I couldn't imagine going anywhere. Whatever my life underwater held, it was nothing like this. I didn't need my memories to know that.

Chapter Eleven

WRINDEL

MY MERMAID. My princess.

It felt so damn good just to be close to her, to be inside her. It all felt so new, though I was glad for my experience, that I knew how to make this good for her. I made sure to keep her little clit stimulated, stroking it with my finger here and there to make her mewl, and then pulling back again to keep her in suspense. Her nipples got the same treatment. I took my time with her, because I wanted it to be incredible. I wanted her to come like a meteor hitting the earth.

I pushed her legs up so I could rub the soles of her feet. I had a feeling her skin was very tender there. It seemed to shock her system to touch the newborn shape of her legs and feet. It made her a little uncomfortable, too.

But that was the beauty of it. A little surprise, a little pain—it was the seasoning in the stew.

Sure enough, the combination of my cock pumping into her and my hands running along the sensitive arches of her feet and tugging on her toes seemed to render her speechless. Her hair was spilled across the bed. She made little sounds that were not quite words.

That was how I brought her to climax the first time. Her pussy tightened hard around me, her muscles convulsing, her whole body shuddering, her moans completely unbidden. I was on the brink of losing all control, gripping her ass, groaning deep as I lost myself inside her.

Usually in this moment, I felt pleasure and relief. But this was different. This was a primal urge to fuck as hard as I could, to make babies with this girl, to keep her so close and so aroused that she never thought of anything but me. When I started to come, I was rougher with her than I meant to be. It almost didn't even feel good. It was too strong.

She didn't try to stop me, though.

When I was done, I was almost dizzy with it. Breaking apart was agony. I never wanted to be apart from her.

She was breathing hard, looking into my eyes. She found my hand and laced my fingers with hers.

"Wrindel," she said. "That was beautiful."

"Talwyn." I put my hand on her cheek. I didn't know how to put it in words. She had to stay. I had to keep her here.

She smiled, closing her eyes, our fingers still interlocked all through the night.

"FATHER WANTS TO SEE YOU," Ithrin told me the next morning while I was enjoying breakfast with Talwyn in my private quarters. Taking her to dinner had been hasty, I realized. Today, I planned to show her the rest of the palace and take her out in the carriage for a tour of the town.

"Right now?" I rose reluctantly. "Is he all right?"

"He's doing a little better today, actually."

"Go ahead," Talwyn said. "I can wait here."

"If he's going to tell me to send Talwyn away, I'm not doing it," I said.

Ithrin just stood by the door, looking as if my stalling tired him.

Well, it wasn't like I could refuse Father anything when he was sick in bed.

Coward, I told myself. Because in the end, Father wouldn't make me send Talwyn away. I knew that. I really just hated visiting him in his sickbed.

I had always been terrified of sick people. Even though I was a baby when Mother, Jiriel and Seldana were dying, maybe early memories lurked in my mind. Or maybe I was just an irresponsible cad after all.

I didn't like problems I couldn't fix. When you're a prince, you can't make the whole kingdom happy, but at least you can grant a lot of favors. You can benevolently purchase a loaf of bread for a begging child. When you see the owner of a tavern beating a poor serving girl for a simple mistake, you can offer her a job in the palace kitchens. When your older brother is in a brooding mood, you can force him to go have a night out.

I couldn't do a damn thing for Father. I couldn't ease his pain. I couldn't figure out what was wrong. I could only listen to his abruptly weakened voice and look into his face, which was so much like an older version of Ithrin's and mine, but ghastly pale.

"Father?" I entered the room. A window was open for fresh air but the fireplace was blazing to counteract the cool breeze. A dozen bottles littered the table, and the air smelled thickly of medicines.

"Sit down, Wrin. I need to make sure I say these things before I go."

"Go?" My stomach wrenched. "Ithrin said you were feeling better today."

"A little, but what does that mean? Nothing. Your mother was unconscious with fever for two days, then perfectly lucid, barely even coughing, for three hours before she died. Just long enough to find out that Jiriel and Seldana had already died the day before. This is it, I feel it. Maybe it will take two days, maybe two months, but I'm leaving this earth."

"You're only eighty! Have they said what's wrong?" I waved at all the medicine bottles. "Are all these here just for *show?*"

"I don't know why, but we just don't live long, do we?" He smiled wryly. "Some elves we are. But such is life. As they said, elves live for two centuries, as long as we eat good food, drink clean water, and never leave our houses. I didn't follow that advice, did I? I suppose it's caught up to me."

"*Damn.*" I slammed my hand on the bedside table so hard that one of the bottles jumped off, but I caught it. I turned it over, my eyes unfocused as I stared at the label. "I don't even know what to say. You've always been there for me…"

"I don't want to go," he said. "I wanted to see your children. But…I have to believe I will never leave your side. I know our lost loved ones never left us. I see your mother in my dreams all the time…"

I wasn't as sentimental as Father. I didn't have as much faith. I tried to think it was true but instead I was just furious.

"Wrin," he said. "About this mermaid of yours…"

"Ithrin told you?"

"Well, the whole castle is talking about it, obviously. Just because I'm in bed doesn't mean I've gone deaf."

"I know. Grandfather had a shameful dalliance with a mermaid, and now history must repeat itself, I suppose. No one will consider that things might be different for us."

"It was long before my time," Father said. "Long before he married my mother. I was well into adulthood before anyone told me about it. But aside from him, I'm sure you know how these things always end. You know the spell that forces a mermaid to the land. I want you to be with the woman you love, same as your brother, but mermaids are not of this world. You can't have her without a lie."

"It's just one lie," I said.

"You can't love someone and lie to them. Not about something like that."

"I don't want to lie. But if I tell her the truth, she will change back, even if she wants to be with me. And she does. In this case, the truth would hurt her."

"But what are you taking from her?"

Her sisters. A lump sat in my throat. Talwyn loved and protected her sisters and I had to tell her that we never talked about our families. I knew it was wrong for me to keep her from remembering them, but damn it all, they were also adults. They could find their own way. They surely wouldn't stay so close forever. Ithrin was terribly important to me. But in the end, wasn't one's true love more important than sisters?

My own inner arguments didn't sit right, yet I had no idea what else to do.

"You never got to see my marriage with your mother," Father said. "I hope I've told you enough that you can make the right decision."

Talwyn would choose me. She would stay on land, keep her legs. I am as sure as I've ever been of anything.

Chapter Twelve

Talwyn

When I was left alone, I abandoned breakfast (I was still not sure what I thought of bread, such a very dry food) and carefully made my way to the balcony. My steps were shaky but I was able to walk. Outside Wrindel's quarters, an elegant ribbon of water-fall fell into a shallow pool. I sat down and slipped my feet into the water. The cool liquid felt like home, but it didn't seem right. This water had no salt, no fish, no plants lining the ocean floor, just pristine crystal liquid, shimmering in the sunlight.

A yearning came over me. I couldn't deny how happy I had been last night. I felt sure I had never experienced such joy as in Wrin's arms. But mornings had a sobering quality.

Who was I leaving behind?

When Wrin came back, I could tell he was shaken from the visit with his father.

"Are you all right?"

"All right," he growled. "Am I all right? Is he all right? That's all anyone asks anymore. What am I supposed to say? He thinks he's dying. Maybe he's right. Our family has never had good luck with...living."

My chest tightened.

He softened. "Don't worry, sunshine. I don't want to think about it. Let's have a day on the town. You seem to be walking all right, if I give you my arm for balance?"

"I think so." I was eager to see more of this world. "But will we ride on the horse again? I'm not sure I can handle it."

He laughed. "We'll take a carriage."

If I could use one word to describe the day that followed— well, no single word could ever be enough. It was magnificent and overwhelming and astonishing. The carriage was a neat little box with windows, that rattled down the roads. Wrindel warned that it might make me feel sick, but it didn't. The rocking reminded me of rough waters. And that carriage brought us around the entire city.

I saw more buildings and people in one day than I had seen in all my years traveling the seas. Wrin showed me the massive water wheel that powered a mill, the great fish market where the best of the day's catch was sold in a clamoring frenzy called an auction, and the hills of grape vines that made elvish wine. I couldn't get enough of all the sights, the different styles of cloth-ing, the animals.

It was an incredibly hectic world up here, noisy and dirty with the constant clink of coins, the shouting of street vendors. I would be lying not to admit I also saw things that disturbed me. Some of the people looked very lean and hungry, and I saw a woman hit a crying child and a man in a wooden cage that was strung up in a tree being jeered at by children. Wrindel said he was being punished for stealing, and I went pale.

He laughed. "You won't be punished for stealing Kiara's compact."

But it was a sobering thought.

"This world is very serious at times, isn't it?"

"What do you mean? Every world is serious at times."

"Well—you have such valuable possessions and grand dwellings. So the stakes are higher for everything."

"Yes...everyone wants something more," he said.

"The Great Temptation," I murmured. "I think I understand it now."

"What is the Great Temptation?"

"It's what the merfolk call yearning for surface world things. They think it's dangerous, almost like a sickness."

"You mean to tell me most mermaids don't yearn for anything?"

"They seem like they don't. It's hard to remember details, but I think they always sneered at me for scavenging."

"Did they ever buy the things you scavenged?"

"Of course they did."

He snorted. "Of course they did, indeed." He took my hand and squeezed it. "I think it's good to yearn for things, myself. It keeps you alive."

Some tightness loosened within me, that I had hardly known was there. I had always been ashamed of wanting to see new things and meet different sorts of people. Here, it was no longer a sin.

When the sun was sinking lower, Wrindel took me up a hill outside the city proper, to a formation of ancient stones. Some were twice as tall as I was; most set in a circle, but others placed apart. I was confident enough on my feet by now that I wandered around them, trailing my fingers on the rough texture of the stones. The light set everything aglow.

"You can find circles like this all over the land," he said. "They align with movements of the sun. Elves and the fair folk still worship the old gods here when the seasons turn. We'll have festivals here, then. But I think it's beautiful on a quiet evening when no one's here."

"I saw something like this under the ocean once," I said.

"Built by merfolk?"

"No, in the Flooded Lands. To the south. There is a town under the water. The merfolk don't built anything very impressive, but they have dozens of sea gods," I said. "They're different every fifty miles or so."

"They? Don't you mean 'we'?"

"Maybe. But I never felt a part of things. In the end, all the gods are the same anyway, don't you think?"

"Oh, now what would be the fun in that?" he said. "I think they're different, but well acquainted." He winked at me. "C'mere, I want you to see something else before the sun goes down." He led me to an outcropping of rocks, and when I climbed up after him I realized I could see the entire city from here, rooftops glowing golden and spires glinting all the way to the endless ocean beyond as the sun was sinking below the horizon.

"I never realized that you could see so much from the top of a hill!" I looked down and glimpsed a terrifying drop off, and took a quick step back, losing my balance.

Wrindel caught me before I could fall. "Careful, sunshine. You're all right."

"I feel like a god myself," I said. "Seeing the whole city at once. We're higher than birds!" I said, noticing a tern flying below us. I met his eyes. "This has been the most wonderful day..."

"Well, I wanted to show you that the pleasures of Wyndyr— and becoming my princess—aren't limited to the bedroom," he said. "There's a whole world to show you. A lifetime of delights."

"Oh, Wrin, I so want to stay."

"Then stay." He tipped up my chin and gave me a chaste kiss on the lips. It was very courtly. The kiss I gave him in return was a little less so.

"I'm glad I'm not a human," he said. "Their gods don't like love-making in church. But the old gods are a randy lot and it's good luck to practice a little fertility worship..."

"Maybe they'll bless us with a child." The words slipped out of my mouth, as if the place had bewitched me. A child? Where had *that* come from?

His face warmed, the lust in his eyes softening into something more, and I blushed. "I mean—I said that before I thought. It's...it's too soon for that. I don't know if we can even... I mean, if I became a mermaid again, what would happen?"

"We'll deal with that if it arises," he said. "But nothing would make me happier, Tal, not in the whole wide world. It's not likely, though. My parents didn't have their first child until ten years of trying, and my grandparents had the same trouble."

"Good," I said. "I can throw caution to the wind." My body yearned for him to fill me again, to feel the caress of his hands and mouth all over my newly born form. I'm sure I could not have resisted if I tried, and if it pleased the gods and it pleased us, what could be the harm?

Chapter Thirteen

TALWYN

ANOTHER MORNING BROUGHT another sobering reminder of my situation. I wondered how long this would be my lot—to wake up confused and concerned, then to forget all about it as the day progressed. Wrindel summoned two healers to see me, a man and a woman, both tall and white-haired. They examined my head.

"I see no signs of injury," the woman said. "But it could have been internal. What is your name, dear?"

"Talwyn."

"Your age?"

"Twenty-three."

"She's older than you, your highness. You'd better listen to her," the man joked.

"I don't listen to people just because they're older than me. Ask Ithrin."

"Where were you born?" the woman continued.

"That...I don't know," I said. "But I'm not sure I ever did. I was born in the sea, but I couldn't tell you the village. My mother—" I started to speak, as if I remembered her, and then stopped short when I realized that I didn't.

"I think her memory loss is magically induced," the woman said. "You can tell the memories are there. Magic is blocking them."

"I feared as much," Wrindel said. "And there's nothing you can do?"

The woman paused, looking at me strangely. "No."

Wrindel saw them out the door before turning back to me. I was sitting stiffly in his bed, feeling like I had failed some sort of test. "I'll never get my memories back? I can never return to the sea?"

"Is that so bad? You want to stay here with me, don't you?"

"I—I do. But I'm worried about my family."

"Tal—" He hesitated. "Of course you are. I could put out inquiries to the other merfolk..."

"Are you keeping something from me?"

He paused. "I have to."

"Why?"

"If I told you, you would have to leave. You could never return to this world. I need to keep you safe."

"I don't understand! You're lying to me?"

"No!" he barked. "It's part of the curse. I have to lie to you, and you need to keep from poking into the truth, because you would lose me and I'd lose you. You have to trust me."

I rubbed my arms. This made me very nervous. "But...my family. If I could just talk to the merfolk..."

"You can never go to the shore again," he said, his words coming more painfully. "It's too dangerous."

"Never? I can never—swim in the ocean?"

"The palace is full of places to swim."

"This woman wants to keep me from the ocean," I said. "She must be my enemy. Maybe she wants to hurt my family! I have to protect them."

"I don't think she wants to hurt your family. I think she only wanted to deliver you to me."

"How do you know? Why?"

"That...I'm not sure."

"What kind of answer is that?"

"I'll ride down to the docks right now and take my ship out to signal the merfolk. I'll find out what's become of your family. I swear it. I can't lose you." He grabbed a cloak and rushed out the door.

When he was gone, I stomped around the room. Stomping was new to me. It was rather satisfying. Last night had been so beautiful, and now it was spoiled beyond repair. I knew that this wasn't his fault; I believed he wanted my happiness above all else, but how could I stay without knowing? And even if he did find out the situation with my family, how could I live without ever feeling the ocean water again? This choice was so terrible, I didn't know how I could make it.

Someone knocked on the door.

"Talwyn? It's Ellara," a voice called.

I opened Kiara's compact and checked my appearance, straightening out my hair and forcing a smile onto my face. "Come in."

"Good morning. Wrindel told me I should make sure you're all right..." She was dressed simply in a gown of pale blue cotton edged with lace, and held something cupped in her hands. "I brought you a mouse, if you want it. If they scare you, I'll take it away, but it's my magic to tame them, and I think they're cute."

"What is a mouse?"

"See?" She opened her hands. She was holding a small, furred creature with tiny round ears and even tinier feet. It sniffed the air tentatively and then squeaked.

"Oh, it is cute!"

"Do you want to hold her?"

Ellara passed the mouse to my outstretched hands. It climbed into my palm and lifted its head to me.

"She wants to be petted," Ellara said. "Like this." She stroked the mouse's head with one finger.

"Ah, it's so soft." I was charmed despite my distress. "We don't have furry things underwater."

"I can bring a little bed in and she'll sleep by the fire. It's just too cute when they do that. Ithrin doesn't quite get how I can spend fifteen minutes just watching a mouse sleep." Ellara smiled and then she noticed Kiara's compact. "Is that—? Did you steal that from her?"

I nodded.

Ellara burst into laughter. "She never goes without that thing! Of course, she's probably already bought a new one, but—" She shook a finger at me. "You're all the trouble she was hoping I'd be."

"She hoped you'd be trouble?"

"Goblins have a reputation for it," Ellara said. "We steal things, too, traditionally. But I've been good. I'm half-elf after all, and I don't want to embarrass Ithrin. I know Kiara's been hoping to catch me at something, though."

"I'll give it back to her," I said. "Just not yet. If...I stay here at all." I looked at her. "Ellara, can I ask you something?"

"Of course."

"I have to choose. Either Wrindel, and the sea and all my memories."

"Ithrin told me," Ellara said.

"What would you do?"

"How can I possibly answer for you? From my perspective, it would be easy. Most of my memories aren't very good. It *would* kill me to forget Father, but I know he wouldn't want me to choose the memory of him over my future. Of course, I've never had to choose between entire worlds."

"I think I'm happier here," I said. "But I can't just consider my own happiness. I think...I left someone behind."

"Why don't we go to the library?" Ellara said.

"Is there a book about mermaids who turn into humans? Wrin has a book with a picture of a mermaid by his bed..."

"He was reading some legends," Ellara said. "But maybe we can find a true account. There is a book for absolutely *everything* in the palace library. You won't even believe it."

She was right. My mouth gaped open like a fish as we entered the room. In the front of the room were several large tables beneath a skylight. Behind them, books lined all the walls on every side of the long and very tall room. The spines were all sorts of colors, some with gold, some books thick and so tall that I would have struggled to pull them off the shelf, many of them bound in leather. Ornate ladders were attached to the shelves and rolled on wheels. A man was at the top of one of them, putting the books back on the shelf.

And in the center of the room were drawers and racks that held scrolls and huge individual papers—mostly maps, Ellara said—and collections of letters and documents.

"Where do we even begin? How do you find anything in here?"

"It's organized," Ellara said. "Either by topic or alphabetically."

"Alphabetically?"

She shrugged. "I'll explain that later. It's a lot to learn if you don't know anything about reading and writing. But all the knowledge of the royal family of Wyndyr is here in this room. Some of the books are a thousand years old. I've spent hours here reading about the elven histories and stuff about court manners and politics, preparing to be queen, especially since the king got sick. If you have a question and the answer isn't here, well..." She threw up her hands.

"So where do we begin?"

Ellara checked the shelf, and then she consulted the locked cases along one wall, which seemed to hold old and fragile books. She had a key for them in her pocket. "The perks of being a princess," she said, with a fanged grin. She quickly found a large stack of material about the merfolk. Her petite form staggered under the weight of them as she heaved them onto a table. I couldn't help because I was still having enough trouble staying balanced on my feet, but she just said, "I do this all the time."

She looked through the first few books. She flipped through the pages so fast I wasn't sure how she knew what she was looking at.

"Oh, I've been reading since I was a child," she said. "You get

very fast at it. I see lots of the usual legends and tales in here...
bits about merfolk life..."

"Like what?"

She read me some selections, and they were mostly wrong.
More nonsense about mermaids laying eggs.

"I don't know if we can trust these books," I said.

"But they all say the same thing about mermaid brides..." Her
eyes skimmed more pages, densely packed with more letters
than I could imagine deciphering. "A man can take a mermaid's
jeweled talisman and she will lose her memories and belong to
him...but if she ever lays a hand on the talisman, she will turn
back into a mermaid." She glanced at me. "Did Wrindel take
something from you?"

"Not that I remember..."

"If he did, he couldn't tell you, or he would lose you."

I frowned. "That fits with what he said earlier. But that
would mean...he stole something from me, knowing he would
steal my memories, too."

"Maybe he didn't know what would happen?"

I gnawed on a ragged edge of my nails. I didn't like this at all.
If Wrindel stole me away from the sea on purpose, to prove to
me that I belonged with him...it wasn't much of a choice he
offered. Not if I could never remember what I'd abandoned.

Ellara cracked open a huge book with hand painted pictures
of mermaids inside. Dust drifted upward and made me sneeze.

"Oh, I don't know these words," Ellara said. "It's some
ancient language."

She turned thick but disintegrating pages. They flecked little
pieces off into her hands. We gazed for a long time at the
pictures, nevertheless. The colors were beautiful and bright, as if
they had been painted yesterday, but the renditions were fairly
crude and often quite strange. Many of the pictures showed life
under the water, but I stopped at a depiction of one mermaid
placing a green stone into another mermaid's mouth. In the next
picture, the mermaid was tied up on the beach, looking
distressed while a man pulled a comb from her hair. On the

facing page, the mermaid had turned into a naked human girl, crawling on the shore with large tears splashing from her eyes while the man stood over her. It looked like she had been traded off against her will.

A story unfolded through the pages. The weeping mermaid had legs and wore a dress. The mermaid and the man were in bed together, with his body on top of hers. In the final picture, she was holding a baby.

"I don't think I want to see this book anymore," I said. "This doesn't seem like a very happy mermaid."

"Well, it has nothing to do with you and Wrindel," Ellara said, but she gave the pictures an uncomfortable last glance before shutting the book again.

An older woman with spectacles came over to us, looking excited. "Yes, that book is a puzzle," she said. "As you can see, the letters are our own, but no one has identified the language. It's one of the oldest books in the library. You can tell by the way the author wrote the letter 'p'. You see, back in those days..." The next five minutes of our lives were occupied by a history of the letter, and I tried not to fall asleep. "Did you need any help?" the woman finally asked.

"I think we're done with this one, actually," Ellara said. "But Miss Pennry...do you have any archives from King Lefior?"

"Of course, we have lots of letters, ledgers and records from all the kings in the history of Wyndyr."

"But we're looking for something in particular," Ellara said. "Anything you might have on the mermaid he kept here at the palace."

Miss Pennry paused. "That was long ago."

"I know it was!" Ellara said, sounding slightly amused. "Come on, it may be a somewhat forbidden topic, but you must have something. You always do."

Miss Pennry seemed begrudging, but she said, "Let me see."

She bustled off through a door, leaving us to keep thumbing through the books in our stack. I fidgeted, starting to grow restless with the words I couldn't read.

And then, Miss Pennry came back with a small, yellowed book. "Take it somewhere else," she said quietly. "And don't tell the king. I think this is what you're looking for, but I'll warn you, it isn't a pleasant tale."

Chapter Fourteen

MARCH 12th

OUR BITTERLY COLD winter seems almost at an end. Today it was warm enough to take a walk by the shore without losing one's nose. I wore a fur-trimmed cloak and fur-lined gloves and two layers of wool on my arms and legs. As I walked, in the distance, I saw an apparition of a girl. A mermaid, sitting on the rocks, hair past her waist and nothing but a string of shells to wear. I tell you, I've never seen anything so beautiful and so strange. When she saw me, she started to sing in that high, haunting voice I sometimes hear off near the rocks of the Wolf's Jaw. But when I came close, she dove into the water.

MARCH 13th

I WENT LOOKING for that girl again. And I found her. She let me get a little closer this time before she disappeared. I don't think she's afraid of me. She always gives me a look almost as if she expects me to follow her. Would that I could.

MARCH 19th

BLESSINGS to the goddess of the water. I finally got close enough to speak to my beauty after a week of days. She was testing me, but it was worth the pursuit. One might think that speaking to her would break the spell she has held over my imagination, but it has not. We must have talked for an hour or more. I was late for the feast with the ambassador from Yirvagna, and even then my mind wandered back to her words.

She is so different from the ladies of the court. Very frank, and wise for her years, with tales of a world I can hardly imagine. For all that, I'd be lying if I didn't admit that it's her lovely face I can't get out of my head. I believe I'd already be looking for a courtship ring if not for her fish tail. Have I fallen in love with a creature of the ocean? That would be torture indeed. No one must know.

MARCH 22nd

WINTER TURNS TO SPRING, and we've had our feasts and revels to celebrate the change of seasons. The court waits with bated breath for me to choose a wife, but once I thought they were drunk enough not to notice, I snuck off to see my Rusa. I brought her a bouquet of tulips, and she said she'd never seen them in all her days.

APRIL 2nd

MY FAVORITE THING in the world is to sneak some object or food off to show her, watch her turn it over in her hands, poke it or taste it. Today I brought her an iced cake. She said it was ghastly. Too sweet. Nothing is so sweet under the sea, she said. Rusa tastes of salt.

APRIL 21st

IT WAS inevitable that someone from the castle would catch me at it eventually. I've now been speaking to my girl for a month of days, and have missed a few appointments. No one understands what a lonely job it is to be the king. Everything is expected of me, every problem laid at my feet, and I have no one to share it with.

What I did not know about Rusa at first is that she is well versed in the art of witchcraft, and the other merfolk turn to her for answers. She can be as pretty and coquettish as any girl of the court, but beneath it all is such a tough and clever mind. She would make me a perfect queen—if she was not bound to the sea.

I have been sleeping very poorly. My subjects have noticed. Today Gairor told me he had seen me with her and informed the rest of the council. They advised me to stop seeing her, as I knew they would, but the one benefit of being the king is that they *cannot* stop me.

MAY 2nd

I HAVE BEEN teaching Rusa to read. It has become nearly unbearable to leave her each day.

MAY 15th

THE SOLUTION WAS before me all this time. I thank the gods for granting me a palace of water! I have brought Rusa home with me, and even as I write she is swimming about in the pool outside my doors. I told her I will not write long so I can read to her the Tale of Jola and Aranath.

MAY 16th

YOU'VE NEVER SEEN SUCH a lot of chattering, cross old crows as my court. They are furious just because I'm happy. They will never let up until I have heirs. I am the most powerful elf in the realm— in the entire world, most likely—and yet my body and my heart are not given choices. If I were a fisherman, no one would give a damn.

MAY 25th

RUSA TAKES to reading like she has been starved for it. She can almost read primers on her own. I am glad of this because so much of life is denied to her. I give her everything within my power, and she endures the snide remarks of the court with excellent humor, but how long will that be enough?

JUNE 2nd

CAN'T SLEEP. My desire is driving me mad. She takes me in her mouth, but I want to take her in my *arms* and know what it is to be deep inside her. I would take her in any form, if I knew any children that resulted would be born elves. I would not subject her to carrying and birthing some twisted half-breed.

JUNE 25th

THE BASIN of water has finally been installed in my box at the theater and last night I took her to an operetta. You can imagine the gossip but I have learned to turn off my ears. Rusa was captivated by the music and she has such an astonishing memory for it that I can hear her right now out my window: "Oh, little bird, why do you sing when you are so sad?"

JULY 14th

UNCLE VIRNAN CAME to visit and "discuss" Rusa with me. He begged me to send her back to the ocean this very day. He said it is better "for her" to end it now before it goes too far. It would be incredibly painful for her now; we go to the theater three days a week and she reads a book or two every day. She has adapted to my world and it would be cruel to send her back now.

JULY 25th

DESPITE IT ALL, this has been the happiest summer of my life.

JULY 28th

SHE SAYS I don't listen to her concerns, and that I don't stand up to the rest of the court on her behalf.

How can she make such accusations? All I do is listen to her concerns. They consume me. I hardly know who I was before I met her. She has no idea of what pressures I face. She is quick to remind me, after all, that merfolk do not have nearly so many rules and expectations.

JULY 29th

WE HAVE HAD a good talk and spent all night reading the Song of the White Stag together. I shouldn't write here when I'm upset.

The wolvenfolk have been making a lot of trouble in the northern forests again. Gairor is urging me to take a trip to Mardoon to discuss a joint organization of our patrols. I don't want to leave Rusa.

SEPTEMBER 10th

CAN'T SLEEP. I have just gotten back from Mardoon and Rusa looks so pale and ill. The healers say she can't live long in these waters. I want to believe they're lying to me, but the proof is right before my eyes. If I were to be responsible for her death, I would never forgive myself.

There is some hope: in Mardoon, I heard a story of "shore-stones", which can grant a mermaid legs. They are very rare but I'd pay any price to have one. I have ordered my men to go looking for one, but I know they are reluctant. No one wants Rusa to be queen.

I would do anything to saddle my horse and scour the countryside looking for one of these shore-stones, but I am the king. I must stay. And what would become of Rusa in my absence?

SEPTEMBER 20th

PRINCESS INTARA of the Luwin Isles is here, and everyone has been trying to urge us together. I must confess that she is a pretty and very sharp witted girl and I spent longer talking to her than I should.

But it is Rusa I want, Rusa I cannot have. She is close to me, but always elusive. The longer she is here, the more elusive she seems. She has changed. She was once so frank with me, so interested in everything. Now, more often than not, she sits quietly in her pool. If the shore-stones can't be found, I fear I will have to let her go.

OCTOBER 16th

ONE OF MY scouts has returned and says he has found a necklace of shore-stones. We must find out how to use them, but—

There is hope!!

The most precious happiness is so close I can taste it. I dare not make a bet on it until I see that it works, but if it did, oh gods. I would marry her tomorrow.

OCTOBER 18th

THE SCHOLARS HAVE BEEN COMBING through the archives, trying to find how to use the shore-stone, and they believe they have found an answer. There is a picture in an ancient book. She must swallow the stone. I think it might just work. The book seems to know its business.

Legends of mermaid brides agree that she will lose all her memories of her life before. That is the only trouble. But I don't think Rusa had much of a life before.

"THE NEXT ENTRY COMES MUCH LATER," Ellara said. "'It has been four years now since Rusa vanished in the night. It all seems like a dream, now. A bad dream? No. Despite it all, a good one. Rusa always was, and always will be, a beautiful dream to me...but I understand now that I wronged her. I tried to imprison her in a world where she could never belong. Princess Intara will be my bride, but Rusa remains my love.'" Her eyes kept skimming the page. "He writes a confession, here. It's quite long and despairing. The poor man must not have had anyone to talk to."

"That is...so sad."

Ellara sighed. "Forbidden love! But what happened to the shore-stone? It didn't work? It seems so unfair."

"I think it did work," I said. "It was too late. She had grown resentful of being imprisoned in a little pool of water. She didn't want to lose her memories."

"I don't why you have to lose your memories. True love conquers all."

"Well, I don't have my memories," I said.

"I still say there must be a way to be together without it being so horrible. I mean, what is the point of such frustrating magic?"

"If only we knew."

Deep down, I felt I knew what had happened. Worst of all, I understood it. It was already eating at me, wondering what my life under the sea had been. Would that feeling grow over months and years?

It would not be Wrindel's fault. He hadn't made the rules. He didn't like the rules. If I knew what I was getting into, I sensed I probably would choose him instead of my life under the water.

But not knowing...

I needed to find my family. I couldn't rest without *knowing*. Wrindel would never let me go to the shore, but I would have to take the risk.

Chapter Fifteen

WRINDEL

I WALKED the shore for hours, calling for Rusa. At one point, I thought I heard an eerie song, but I never saw movement on the rocks or in the waters. It might have been the wind. I was so hoarse from screaming over the crashing waves that by the time I straggled back to the palace, I sounded like I had laryngitis.

I hated to come back with nothing.

"I'm sorry, Tal. I didn't find anything out today, but I will."

I had never seen such concern in her eyes. "It's all right...," she said. "I have this feeling you never will find anything out..."

"What makes you say that?"

"It's a choice I must make. I can't have my memories and you, all at once. And I know that you are the one I would choose..."

But the way she trailed off made me wonder. It was not as simple as that.

That night, she was still my alluring sea-maiden as she shed her clothes and sprawled naked on the bed. She still pressed herself against me and spread her legs for me. But I sensed that it was a tender love making she wanted tonight. I was gentle with her, running my fingers through her hair and caressing every inch of her skin, trying to show her as best I could without words that I loved her. I loved her and I would never let her down, never make her sorry for what she had sacrificed.

I had never felt before like I failed with a woman. And no doubt, I made her shiver and laugh with pleasure that night.

But I still felt I had failed her. Somehow or other.

Lies and lost memories hung between us like a tangled mass of cobwebs.

Two weeks passed by in a whirl and I filled them with more delights, as if I could distract us both from our troubles forever. I finally dared to bring Talwyn back to dinner. As soon as she walked in, Kiara's eyes were on her, and full of loathing that had probably only grown after two weeks of court gossip.

Talwyn walked right up to her and handed her the compact. "I've been meaning to return this to you."

"You! You stole my compact?"

"Mm-hm," Talwyn agreed brazenly. "I did."

Kiara's mouth snapped open with momentary speechlessness. Clearly she had expected an excuse. "Why?"

"Because you called me 'fishy', and insulted me, and Ellara too, while you were at it."

"And that makes it all right to steal from me?"

"No, but it does make it understandable, doesn't it? I'm sure you agree that we both behaved immaturely." Talwyn offered a hand. "I stole it in a moment of impulse. I don't want to quarrel with members of Wrindel's court."

Kiara looked quite appalled at this gesture. I think she had expected to be sniping back and forth with Talwyn for years to come, and probably would have preferred it that way. I had to laugh. It was actually brilliant to get the upper hand. Talwyn had excellent instincts for making the court follow her lead instead of the other way around. Kiara reluctantly shook fingertips with Talwyn. She sat down and exchanged grins with Ellara. When Ithrin sat down, Ellara whispered about it to him, and he nodded at Talwyn.

We really feel like a family again, I thought.

The only misfortune was that Father's chair remained empty.

And not halfway through the soup course, the main healer entered the room abruptly. "I apologize for the intrusion," he said with a bow, and then he approached Ithrin. He was moving stiffly, his brow creased with lines of concern that didn't budge. "It's the king," he said. "You should both see him now."

The soup churned in my stomach as we shoved our chairs back. The girls stayed behind; Ellara would watch over Talwyn. My heart was thumping. *Is this it, then? Is this how we lose Father? He slips away during dinner just as the family fortunes are finally turning?*

For all the times Ithrin and I had argued, I was glad for him now. Sometimes I found him steady and strict, but this very quality served him well now. I was not prepared for how wrecked Father looked, his head collapsed on his pillow, his breath labored.

I wanted to rage at the healers by his bedside. *Why haven't you fixed this?* I turned my fury toward Ithrin instead, but it was meant for them to hear. "I don't understand how he could be dying from an ailment no one can diagnose! He's the king! We have some of the best healers!"

"It happens, Wrin," Ithrin said. His patience was pained. "Healers can't make miracles. It's Jiriel and Seldana all over again."

"I'm sorry," Father said. "You boys have already endured so much..."

"Don't apologize," Ithrin said. "Save your strength."

Father took our hands in his, which had grown thin in a matter of weeks. He didn't seem to have the strength to say anything more for a little while. What was there to say? How do you say goodbye when all you want to do is rage at fate? Elves usually had at least one parent left on their century-day. Ithrin and I were not yet thirty and we were about to be orphans.

"I don't want to dwell on sadness now," Father finally said, as if sadness could be helped. "Bring your girls in to see me."

"Both of them?" I asked.

"I want to see your mermaid. History be damned. If she makes you happy, I will be happy. If I must die, I want to die thinking that you will not be alone."

Father was as good as giving me his blessing to marry Talwyn. I hadn't realized what a weight that was until it was gone. "I'll get her now."

We returned to the dining room, only to be told the court had retired to the music room. Before we made it there, we bumped into Ellara, who was dashing down the hall. She reeled back when she saw us, almost turning a circle. Then she hid her face.

"I'm so sorry," she cried. "I lost her!"

"What do you mean, you lost her?"

"I mean—Talwyn—she disappeared. When you two left, everyone started getting up and talking about the king's health, and it was sort of a commotion and—I realized that Talwyn was gone. I already checked the privy, and your bedroom..."

"It's not *your* fault," Ithrin said, running a hand over her curls. "Either she was kidnapped...or there is something she intends to do."

"Not kidnapped. I think she's gone back to the sea." I started to run.

I knew what I had to do.

Chapter Sixteen

TALWYN

I PICKED my way carefully down the steps from the palace to the path leading toward the shore, holding the hem of my dress high. I would hurry, before anyone worried too much that I was gone. The last thing I wanted to do was hurt Wrindel when his father was dying. But I had to know.

As soon as I reached the beach, I nudged off my shoes. The rocky shore was painful on my sensitive feet, but the kiss of salt water on my skin was like coming home.

I reached the waves, which crashed on the rocks in the moonlight. I looked out at the endless expanse of water before me, at the shadowed depths, and I missed it so much that tears sprang to my eyes.

I had never appreciated its beauty, had I? I wanted more...all the time, more. I was never satisfied with the primal flow of tides and currents. I thought the sea offered me nothing compared to the land. But seeing it again, I understood all at once that it was simply a different kind of existence, with its own kind of beauty.

I lifted my voice into the high song of the sea, "*Hello*!" I didn't know the names of my family, but I felt in my bones that they must be waiting for my return.

It didn't take long before two sleek heads bobbed up in the waves. One of them waved an arm at me. Then they swam forward as I started to walk toward them, my skirts dragged back and forth among the seaweed and foam.

"Talwyn! Talwyn!" They cried my name, two mermaid girls, grabbing me around the waist. I crouched down and hugged them. They looked like me.

"Sisters..." I was crying. "I've lost my memories, but I knew you were waiting for me. I'm so sorry."

"That elven man stole you away! Talwyn—thank gods you came back. We traded away our hair to get a spell that would save you."

"Oh, girls..." I realized they did look...different. Which was strange to say, when I didn't quite remember them. But when they told me they had sold their hair, I understood immediately. I remembered their faces, but they had not looked so stark, with their hair cropped close.

One of them—the slightly older one—put a shell into my hand. "Open it," she said. "Hurry."

I felt torn in two. Seeing them, feeling the ocean water swirl around my legs, a part of me wanted nothing more than to take the spell. But this was my past. Wrindel was my future. The way we talked, the pleasures we shared... No matter how painful it was to turn my back on my home, I still wanted to wake up beside him for the rest of my life more than I wanted anything.

"I—I don't know," I said. "I don't want to abandon you. I want to be your sister, forever and always. But—"

"Talwyn, please! You don't belong there. You'll never be happy on the surface. Rusa said—"

"Rusa?"

"The healer witch."

"Rusa," I repeated. "The witch is *Rusa*..." I clutched my head. "If I could only remember—!"

"Take this shell and you *will* remember." My sister curled my hand around the shell. "Please, Tal. How can you ever be our sister again if you don't even remember the lives we shared? You've raised us since we were little kids."

"I will always be your sister. I remember your faces. I know that I love you. But...there is something else I need to remember." I couldn't remember it, but I knew how important it was. A missing piece of Rusa's story. A piece I needed, no matter what I had to sacrifice.

Wrindel...I'm so sorry.

I cracked open the shell.

A flash of white hot magic blinded me. A searing pain shot up my legs, and all at once I felt them fusing together. I fell toward the rocks, and I would have surely scraped myself or worse if my sisters hadn't caught me.

The silver flash of my tail was like seeing an old friend again —I had never gotten used to the sight of toes!—but I wasn't sure it felt right anymore. All the delicious sensations that Wrindel had teased out of me—I might never feel it again. Like Rusa, even if Wrindel wanted to make love to me in this form, he never could. We would not take the risk of having children who didn't fit in either world, who were cruelly disfigured in ways we could have prevented.

And what was it all for?

I remembered now.

Chapter Seventeen

WRINDEL

I KNEW WHAT I WANTED, and I knew what was right.

I held the necklace in my hands, the stone warming to my skin as I gripped it tight, as I charged down the stairs to the sea.

This decision would never be easy. I knew I might break Talwyn's heart, as I broke my own. But Father was right—we could never marry under the shadow of a lie. She would always wonder about what she had left behind to be with me. And keeping her past a secret, keeping her from her sisters, would tear at my conscience over time.

Maybe we could find another way to be together, another spell…one that didn't force us into a lie. If not…

I would have to accept it, even if the thought was like swallowing a shard of glass.

My boots hit the shore. The rocks were black with a slick sheen of reflected moonlight. And she was there, waiting for me, as beautiful as I'd ever seen her—wild blonde hair and a tail of sleek silver. She had shed her elven dress and it sat on the rocks, crumpled like a molted skin.

"Wrin!" she called, her voice catching. "I'm sorry..."

I rushed to her side, letting the stone slip to dangle from my hand. "Don't be sorry, sunshine. I was going to give you this anyway."

"The stone... Why?"

"Because I can't lie to you anymore. You have two sisters whom you've protected since your mother died when you were young. You told me about them. But the witch said I could never let you know. I can't make that choice for you, even if it means we can never be together the way we wish to be."

"Wrin..." Her hands gripped my jacket and collar, as she pulled herself up to embrace me. She clutched me tight. "I don't want to be like Rusa and King Lefior. A prisoner and her captor."

"You know that isn't what I want either. We'll find a way."

"My sisters were here a moment ago," she said. "They had a spell that would break the stone's enchantment. Rusa gave it to them. She wanted to give me to you, so you would fall in love— and then she wanted to snatch me from you. This pain we're feeling...it's her revenge. She was your grandfather's mistress."

"What? But—she would be so old. I can't believe she's even still alive!"

"She is very old. And—before she stole my memories, she told me her side of the story."

"Uh-oh."

"Just—listen." She settled beside me, the two of us sitting on the beach together. My boots were soaked, and a sharp wind ruffled my hair, but I hardly felt the cold. "Ellara read your grandfather's diary to me the other day. It was sort of disturbing, that he kept her in one of those little pools in the palace for so many months. But he taught her to read, and I believe that he really loved her, even though the entire court tried to tell him she was unsuitable. He tried to find the shore-stone that would turn her tail to legs, but when he found it, she left. Her account, however, was different. She felt that he had fallen out of love with her over time, but that whenever she tried to leave, he would plead with her to stay just a little longer. She couldn't really leave without being carried back to the shore, so she felt like a prisoner. Sometimes he neglected her, and when he spent a long evening with the Princess Intara, she felt completely betrayed. When he finally found the shore-stone, he told her she would have to give up all her memories to be with him. She was furious because he acted like this wasn't a big deal, like her life had no importance before she met him anyway."

"So you're just telling me that my grandfather was an ass?"

"No! I think it was more complicated than that. At first, they were both in love. I think she really must have loved learning to read, and having long talks with him by moonlight, and going to the theater. But she could never be a part of his world the way I was a part of yours. I mean, we'll never really know what went on between them, in the end..." She shook her head. "I don't want to judge them. It is their business now. But she did something very, very wicked, in the end. When she heard of the marriage between your grandfather and Princess Intara, she cursed your house."

"Cursed?"

"Yes. She asked for your grandfather's descendants to be plagued with misfortune."

"Is that why my family has been dying? Why we have struggled to have children? That witch? I should have run a blade through her on the bloody spot! If I had *known*—"

She bit her lip. "Wrin, I am so sorry. But this is why I had to take the spell and change back into a mermaid, even if it means I'll lose you. I had this vague sense that she had told me something really important. I am actually so *glad*, in a way, that you were already going to give me the shore-stone back. It makes the decision easier to bear. It was meant to happen, I guess. I was always meant to end up back where I started..."

"Don't say that, sunshine."

She shook her head, as if forcing herself not to succumb to emotion. "I need your grandfather's diary. He wrote a confession in it. An apology to her. I want to show it to her. I'm going to make her break the curse."

"Are you now?"

"Well, I'll try as best I can. Go on, hurry and get that diary!

Ellara knows what I'm talking about. Maybe we can save your father."

She started to push me away, and then she pulled me close instead. She gripped the collar of my jacket and kissed me like it was the last time we would ever see each other. I wanted her more than ever. I couldn't bear to consider that our time together really was at an end.

"I'm going to find a way, sunshine."

Her eyes welled and I knew: to save my father, for Talwyn to see her sisters again, we would both choose the same, even if I never found a way. "Go," she said.

Chapter Eighteen

T ALWYN

M Y SISTERS WERE WAITING for me just offshore.

"Please!" Mirella cried, when I told them my plan. "Don't bother the witch again! She wasn't very nice to us, demanding our hair. What if she does something worse to you this time?"

"I'm sorry," I said. "She cursed Wrin's family. I have to see her. Please—go to the village and spread the word that I'll wait for her at the Wolf's Jaw."

"We're not doing any such thing."

"That witch is going to curse you next! And then what? All you care about anymore is that *man*. You don't care a barnacle for us anymore."

Great. A few weeks without me and my timid sisters had transformed into rebellious, opinionated youths.

"Of course I care about you!" I said. "But you know, girls, maybe it's time to admit that we want different things. You're happy to be mermaids. You want to stay in one place, spend more time in the village, and have more friends there. I don't want to stop being your sister, but I don't want to live in the village. I'd be bored sick. The palace and the sea are so close that if I stayed with Wrindel, we could still see each other all the time. But...if we all kept trying to pretend that we wouldn't rather be doing something else...we wouldn't love each other as much as we do." I pulled them into an embrace. "Someday I'll tell you the whole story of Rusa, and you'll see. It's not a good idea to pretend you're happy being somewhere just because you love someone. Even worse to keep them in a place they don't want to be."

Wrindel brought me the small, precious book that I could not read, wrapped in a shiny waterproof cloth. I couldn't take it underwater. I swam on the surface, holding it above my head. The waves were rough on the surface and knocked me about. The sun was rising by the time I reached the Wolf's Jaw.

When I got there, she was already waiting.

I saw her in the distance, and froze. What was I thinking, trying to demand an old witch remove a curse, based on a grudge she had been holding for two hundred years? Did I think she would read the diary and then shrug and go, *Ah, well, never mind, I understand now.*

I remembered Ellara telling me how elves could be petty because they lived so long.

This isn't going to work. I don't have any magic. I can't make her do anything. She knows I love Wrindel, but no matter how much I beg and plead for her to have mercy on his family, she will only relish it.

But I was the only hope of Wrindel's family, to end the curse that had caused them so much grief. I had to do something.

Rusa might be old, and she might know magic, but her heart is the same as anyone else's. Magic didn't make a person immune to anger, sadness, grief, or heartbreak. I couldn't let her intimidate me. I had to handle her just as I would handle anyone else.

I could hear my mother's voice. *Don't give people what they expect. Give them what they really want.*

I drew closer. She was perched on the tallest rock of the Wolf's Jaw. It was a formation of jutting, sharp rocks that formed a line marching out to sea off the coast of a small Wyndyrian island. Her jewelry gleamed in the rising sun. Her white hair was loose, whipping across her wizened body, and her eyes were locked on me the entire way. The sight of her truly gave me a shudder. I seemed to feel the cold more than I did before.

She expected me to be afraid, so I knew I could not show my fear. What did she want?

Knowing Rusa's story, I think she must have regretted going with the king for her entire life. It probably ate at her. She probably missed reading and the theater and the talks they had once shared. There was no way to make that choice without regret. She probably cursed herself for how it had gone wrong. And that was why she cursed him too.

I could have told her all that from the start, but I'm sure she would have snapped at me. She wouldn't want to admit she was wrong.

All I could do now was tell her that she was *right*. That I had learned something from all of this, that I wanted to learn more. That she was a wise and powerful witch and not a stupid lovesick girl.

"Rusa!" I called up to her perch. "I wanted to thank you."

"Thank me?"

"Yes," I said. "You showed me what I would have if I succumbed to the Great Temptation. I never could understand before what it was just to be. And now I do."

She seemed vaguely confused, and then just as vaguely pleased. "Was he not all you hoped for?"

"In the end, nothing is more important than family. That's what you wanted to teach me, isn't it? You truly are a wise woman."

"Who said I wanted to teach you anything?"

"Then why else did you send me to the land? There is one thing I just didn't get at first. You told me it's easier to be cruel. But I see now, you must have a hard heart to be a witch, isn't that true? You have to make hard choices. You *were* right to leave the king."

"Who are you to judge whether I was right?" She flung

herself off the ledge of the rock and dove into the water beside me. I edged back, trying to protect the book from the splash while hiding a sudden wave of panic. Now she was getting angry. Perhaps I had gone too far when I brought up the king.

"You—you wanted me to know your story, didn't you? You wanted me to understand you, and—and I'm ready now. I want to study magic with you."

I was acting on pure instinct now. What would an old woman want? To be honored and remembered, at the end of her life.

"Magic," she hissed. "All you want is a pretty elven man."

"I want a lot more than a pretty elven man. I always have."

"You've never shown yourself to have any desire to learn magic from me. You think you'll win me with flattery?"

"Not flattery," I said. "I truly did learn something. And it is all thanks to you. I learned that the Great Temptation goes both ways. That I will never be entirely happy on land or sea. That I will always be torn between Wrindel and my sisters. Is that what you wanted from me? Why else did you do this? You've already cursed the elves. What was your aim?"

"I have no aim. It amuses me."

"I don't believe you."

She pursed her lips. Then she looked down, running her fingers along the stones. For a moment my heart leapt as she touched the necklace of shore-stones. *Yes,* I thought. *Give me another shore-stone. Let me go back to him!*

"He loved you," I said. "His descendants have suffered because of your curse."

"He *loved* me? I suppose that's what they told you."

"I know you can read," I said. I handed her the book. "This is Lefior's diary."

She opened the pages and turned them slowly. She saw hand-writing that must have been familiar to her.

She turned away from me, toward the rock, tilting the pages toward the sun, and read while I waited. Long, tense moments passed. As she read, her breathing caught with emotion.

Then, she demanded, "You read this?"

"Princess Ellara read it to me."

"So, I suppose you think that's love. Realizing, years later, after he's married someone else, that he wasn't fair to me. He didn't *love* me. He thought I was beautiful and unusual, and I was his way of defying a life that chafed at him. He wouldn't let me go, but he had complete control over when I saw him and what I could do. He never touched my tail; it was abhorrent to him."

I shook my head, pained at the thought. "I—I understand you, Rusa. I do. You were right to leave. And he was wrong to keep you there. You sent me to Wrindel because you want me to repeat your mistakes, don't you? You want to know you weren't alone; that mermaids and men will always fall into the same trap. It's time to let that go. We can't be happy if we won't admit to ourselves what we really need or want. And I *do* want Wrindel. Wrin is not Lefior, and I am not *you*. Spare Wrindel's father. I will not beg. But I will ask."

She looked at the fading brilliance of the sky as the sun dawned over the city. "I suppose this is the closest I shall ever have to an ending, isn't it? Happy, or otherwise..." Her hands lifted to the back of her neck and unfastened the clasp of one of her necklaces, which held a single smoky gem.

"That is the curse," she said. "It was born of the water, and it will be broken by fire." She slipped the chain into my hand.

"Thank you..." I clasped the stone so hard I could feel the ridges of the setting dig into my skin.

She turned to go.

I probably shouldn't have said anything, but I thought of going back to Wrindel like this, and words spurted out of me in desperation. "Is there—no way then—for me to change back into a human?"

"The spell I gave your sisters broke the enchantment of the shore-stones for you, once and for all. You are a mermaid, and a mermaid you will remain."

I sucked in a furious breath. "But—"

"This is what you wanted, isn't it? You were willing to make this sacrifice to break the curse. Bring it to your prince. His father will live a good long life. If you love him that much, there are many pools in the Palace of Waterfalls to accommodate you."

I cursed, and Rusa laughed like this pleased her. Then she slipped under the water, taking the diary with her, to be water-logged and ruined.

Cruel to the end. If breaking the curse worked, then I supposed I had "won", but it felt like a hollow victory.

Chapter Nineteen

W<small>RINDEL</small>

I HAD sentries posted at the water to watch for Talwyn, while I kept vigil over my father's deathbed with Ithrin. He had slipped into unconsciousness.

My life was drawn into a tight focus. All my years of dallying had not brought me as much happiness as these weeks with Talwyn. I clenched my hands on the carved arms of my chair, remembering how I felt when I made love to Talwyn—like I wanted her so badly that it was almost a torture, even though she was right there in my arms. If I let her go, I knew I would imagine her face, and her voice, attached to every other woman I ever knew.

This was love, and it was crueler than I could have ever guessed.

"Prince Wrindel!" One of my sentries spoke breathlessly after opening the door without even knocking. He should have been reprimanded for that, probably, but right now no one cared. "Talwyn returned and she asked me to give you this." He held a necklace.

I stepped outside with him, so I wouldn't disturb my father. Ithrin and Ellara, who had been waiting with me, followed. "What is this?" I asked.

"She says it must be thrown into a hot fire and that will end the king's sickness. My apologies for bursting in, your highnesses."

"This is urgent," Ithrin said. "The kitchen staff will be up and getting their fires hot. We can take it down there."

"Did Talwyn say anything else?" I asked.

"No, your highness. But I think she is there still."

"We can take care of the necklace," Ellara said. "Why don't you go see her?"

Ithrin gave me a concerned look and clapped my shoulder. He was trying to be comforting, but it didn't work at all, because his eyes said, *I'm sorry. You love her, don't you, you poor bastard?*

"I suppose you think it serves me right for all my lack of responsibility," I muttered.

"I didn't say anything," Ithrin said.

I rushed out, my wet boots squelching down the stairs. I had not dared take the time to change them.

Talwyn was sitting on the beach, looking out toward the water, her fingers working tangles out of her hair, but as I came close, she turned to me.

I sat down beside her. Now the seat of my trousers was wet, too. But I just didn't care.

"You got the necklace, right?" she asked.

"Ithrin and Ellara are throwing it into the fire right now."

"Wrin...I'm sorry. I think this is it. Rusa said the shore-stones won't work on me anymore. I'm stuck like this..."

"Stuck? No. You are what you are, sunshine."

"A fish?" She rubbed her eyes. "I want to be with you."

Talwyn and I had gotten to know each other out here on the shore, just like this. At the time, I tried not to let myself admit I was falling for her. We were too different, I thought.

She didn't seem different to me anymore. She was Talwyn. My Talwyn.

"A fish?" I shook my head. "Don't insult yourself. Are the

darklings animals because they have tails? Are goblins beasts because they have horns? No, you're a woman. And I love you."

I pulled her onto my lap, which was very easy, slippery little thing that she was, and kissed her. It was a high bar to say that was the best kiss we'd ever had, but I dare to say it was. It was a kiss with no pretense, no fantasy. She was her true self, and I was my true self, and for all the problems that entailed, I still loved her.

"I love you too," she breathed.

I took her breasts in my hands, teased and tugged at her nipples. "I can still bring you pleasure, can't I, sunshine?" I asked before nipping at her earlobe and trailing kisses down her neck.

I laid her back on the gritty sand. The waves tugged at her hair. I kissed her everywhere, sucking her nipples, licking the saltwater off her neck, sliding my hands down her waist to her hips. She was certainly no fish; her curves were all woman and the skin of her tail was not slimy at all, but supple and soft as silk. I could feel her muscles tensing as I touched her, and then relaxing as I stroked her. She was magic to me, my mermaid, a girl who could live in a world that drowned men.

"Wrin..." She was deeply flushed and I realized how little I cared if she was a human or a mermaid. The sense of wonder and delight I felt around her, the protective hunger she provoked in me, was precisely the same.

"Marry me," I said. "Talwyn, I want you to marry me."

"But...how? What do we do? Rusa and King Lefior tried this path. It only made them miserable. I can't spend my life in some little freshwater pool in the palace. I want to be with you, but it won't work."

"King Lefior kept Rusa in the palace all the time, didn't he? I don't want to keep you. Just...come to me sometimes. You said the merfolk have a season for mating. Ten days out of every two months, something like that? Come to me then."

"But we can't mate. I can't give you heirs."

"Heirs are Ithrin's problem. I just want you. I'll find ways to satisfy you that won't produce any heirs, sunshine."

Her little ears were so pink that I wanted to eat them. "You really...don't care if I'm stuck—I mean, if I'm like this forever?"

"Of course I'm going to keep trying to find a way to bring you back to my world. But—I don't love you for your legs. There's a wide variety of love in the world. I've seen a good bit of it going on at the taverns. Ours can work too. I believe that. I don't want you to live your life feeling regret for what you are because you couldn't be with me. More selfishly, I just don't want anyone else."

"Wrin..." Finally, she broke into a smile. "I'm willing to try."

I carried her back to the palace as the bells of the square were ringing. Those bells rang for holidays and weddings, and I knew what they must mean.

The curse must be broken. My father would live.

Chapter Twenty

TALWYN

WRINDEL HURRIED me up the back stairs of the palace. I was wearing my elven dress, but my fins dangled past the hem, plain to see. The halls were empty here, however. We heard music in the Hall of Marble Pools and people singing, "Hail, hail to the health of the king!"

"Do you think I'll really be allowed to stay here?" I asked.

"That's your doing, sunshine," Wrindel said. "You broke the family curse. Well, not only did you break it, you found out it existed. No one is going to tell you to leave."

He brought me to the pool on the balcony outside his bedroom. Water poured in constantly from a waterfall cascading in from a channel leading from the top floor of the castle, and flowed out into the moat below, so while it might not be as good as sea water, at least it was always clean.

It certainly was small, only about four feet deep and just wide enough that I could swim in a generous circle. But if Wrindel didn't live in a palace full of water, I wouldn't have been able to stay near him at all. And although it wasn't ideal, I was just glad to be close right now. He had stepped back into his room to change out of his wet clothes. Through the glass doors, I watched him strip off his boots. I could see his bed from here. And he could see me, too.

I took off my dress. It wasn't comfortable to wear in the water. He grinned at me and shook his head.

"We might have to get you a little shell top," he said, walking out in bare feet and a clean pair of trousers, buttoning a fresh shirt.

"A shell top? That doesn't sound comfortable."

"That's what mermaids wear in pictures."

"I am not a mermaid in a picture."

"Clearly."

I waved for him to sit down beside me, and covered his hands with mine. "You don't need to button that right now," I said, pushing myself up on the tiled edge of the pool to kiss him. "Although," I realized, "You must want to see your father."

"I do want to see him, and yet...I also don't. I'm glad he's alive. Now I'm afraid he'll have the energy to argue. I asked one of the maids to bring us breakfast before I face that conversation."

A tray of breakfast was delivered shortly. Wrindel brought it out to me, and fixed my coffee with milk and sugar as he knew I liked it. I sat on the edge of the pool so I could keep my tail wet but we could eat together. He knew I didn't really like the sweet breads the elves loved for their breakfast, so we had fruit and glazed ham.

"Not so bad, is it?" he said.

"No, it's quite nice, actually," I said. "But it'll be boring if you're not here. Will you teach me to read?"

"Of course. Although Ellara might be a better teacher."

Someone knocked on the door from within the room. I heard a voice call, "The king is here to see you."

"Already?" Wrindel scrambled to his feet. He quickly threw one of my other dresses at me. "Put that on." He rushed to the door.

I had barely covered up my breasts when the door opened

and the king was brought out to the balcony in a wicker chair with wheels.

"I told 'em I don't need this thing," he grumbled.

Wrindel stood behind him, a little stiff. I supposed we had grown used to living without scrutiny.

"So, you are the one who saved my life," the king said.

"It was somewhat accidental," I said. "But I'm glad you are feeling better."

"Much, much better, yes. Gods, to think that all those years... a bloody curse. That witch ought to hang. But as grateful as I am to be alive, Wrindel is still a prince. I'm a lenient man, but princes can't do *anything* they like."

"Father—"

"What is your intention with her, Wrin?"

"To make her my bride."

"Is she going to change back into a human?"

"I don't know," Wrindel said. "I don't care."

"This is scandalous."

"She *saved* your *life*."

"Your grandfather—"

"Forget Grandfather!" Wrindel snapped. "Talwyn and I have a completely different sort of relationship. She makes me want to work for our happiness. If that feeling isn't love, what is? I think my hardest day with Talwyn will be better than my best day with anyone else."

"I understand that," the king said. "I'm glad to see you caring deeply for someone. But...you may come to regret not having heirs..."

"I already regret a lot of things," Wrindel said. "But I don't think this will be one of them."

"Ah, you're so young..." The king waved a hand. "You don't know your own mortality yet. You don't realize how much you will desire to pass on your line."

"Young, but I have always known loss," Wrindel said. "I think I certainly do know my own mortality. I want children, and so does Talwyn, but if we can only be uncle and aunt, it will have to do."

The king shook his head. "If you're sure, I don't know what I can say. I thought I'd be dead." He gave Wrindel a brief, one-armed embrace. "Don't tell the court I gave my approval. I'd be irresponsible if I didn't try my best to knock some sense into you."

AND THUS IT was all as well as it could be. I stayed for two nights and then I returned to my sisters. My mating season would not begin for several weeks more, and I wanted to make sure my family had been managing without me.

Managing?

I went to our old cave and they weren't there. In the village, I found them living in a stone cottage decorated with coral.

"They said we could live here," Allie said. "An older woman used to live here but she passed on and it's been abandoned ever since. Isn't it adorable?"

"And where is Mirella?"

"She's been fishing with Arilon."

"Who is Arilon?"

"You don't remember him? The big guy with the reddish hair?"

"Oh. Yes. I remember him now." It was so hard to imagine little Mirella, who I used to tell bedtime stories, swimming around with a muscular, gregarious merman. "Well, it seems like you've been doing well."

"I don't know; we've missed you terribly!"

But things had certainly changed in two weeks. It was hard not to feel as if my sisters had been waiting for me to leave! Suddenly they had friends—and a beau, in Mirella's case. They were both working in the village, sprucing up the new cottage. When we had dinner that night, neither of them said a single word about scavenging shipwrecks or trading with human fishing towns.

They didn't miss it at all. I don't even think they realized I expected them to say something about our old lives. They asked me about the Palace of Waterfalls and Wrindel but they seemed entirely satisfied with the arrangement.

But if I was only going to spend one sixth of my days with Wrindel, what would I do with myself? I couldn't see myself spending my days making shell jewelry.

No one had seen Rusa since the night I spoke to her. So while my sisters joined in the social life of the village, I went fishing on my own. Rusa was getting old. Maybe I was crazy to want to spend time with the woman who cursed the elves, but I also had to admit—we had the Great Temptation in common. She understood me.

No one in town knew quite where the old witch lived. She came to them; they didn't go to her. So it took me some days of search, but one day I spotted a soft glow coming from the ancient remains of a shipwreck. It was too old to scavenge. The ship had broken into two when it sank, and was crusted with sea life, but glowfish weren't native to this area. They were traded up the coast from the south; a magic fish that came from a saltwater lake called the Sorcerer's Sea. They could be trained to remain in one place, to permanently light a dwelling.

"Rusa?" I ducked through a decaying window. The glowfish swam toward me like a lonely pet, casting a soft light on glinting jewels.

I gasped as if I'd seen a ghost.

All of Rusa's gems were sitting on the floor of the ship in precisely the arrangement she would have worn them, as if she had laid down and died, and her body had vanished. Where her heart would have been, King Lefior's diary rested.

I knew in my gut that it was a message. I picked up the diary and opened it.

Her voice sang out of the book.

My time has come to leave this world. I shall die alone, as I have lived. Each of my jewels has some power or value. Each was traded to me by some wealthy man in exchange for a mermaid bride. If you have found them, I believe you deserve to have them.

She meant this for me, I knew. I supposed it was a sort of

apology. I slid the bracelets up my arms. I draped jewels around my neck. I stuck the combs in my hair.

I didn't feel more magical. I didn't develop any great powers. When I got home, I even swallowed another damned shore-stone, just in case, but it didn't give me legs.

However, four weeks later, something had happened. For one thing, I had missed my cycles. And strangely, I had an intense craving for sweet bread.

Chapter Twenty-One

T<small>ALWYN</small>

"P<small>REGNANT</small>?" Wrindel looked so happy.

How could he look so happy? We'd agreed that we didn't want this.

"I really think so. All the signs are there. But I'm scared," I admitted, crossing my arms at the edge of the pool. "What if it comes out...wrong...?"

"What if it comes out right?" he said, stroking my hair. "You *want* children. We would have an heir."

"Unless it comes out right...but as a mer. Or what if it had a tail, but it couldn't breathe underwater?"

"I don't know," Wrin said. "I suppose it would die. I don't want to think of that."

His feet were in the water. It was very warm today, maybe the last warm day we would have. I pinched his toes one by one. "You're happy about this and damn the consequences, aren't you?"

"Of course I'm happy, sunshine. You're going to be my wife. I want a family with you, no matter how complicated. What's done is done. Our child will live. The gods blessed us up there on the hill. You said it yourself." He hooked his hands under my arms and pulled me out of the water and onto his lap.

"Tal, I swear to you, we're going to make this work," he said, looking deep into my eyes. "I know it's been strange. I've been getting all kinds of heat for choosing you in the court. Well, when I was burying my sorrows by fucking some courtesan, people admired me as much as they criticized. And what was that? It wasn't healthy and I knew it all along, but I needed something to fulfill me when my family was so fractured. *This* feels right, nothing but right. You and me. I don't care what they say. You don't need to be like me, for us to be together."

A well of intense emotion swept over me. All the time I spent with him before, I wanted so badly to shed my mermaid skin, to get rid of my true form and be like him. I thought it was the only way. When I read King Lefior's diary it only confirmed my suspicions: of course we could not be in love if we were different species!

I had it all mixed up. Being in love didn't mean lying and hiding parts of yourself and trying to be someone you weren't. We could only be in love if we accepted the truth of what we were, and how we felt about each other, and were willing to struggle through all the troubles.

He kissed me, leaning me back onto the painted tiles by the pool. His legs slipped into the water, soaking his clothes, his legs hugging my tail. His erection stroked against me, and gods, I wanted him. I tugged at his hair, dragging kisses across his cheeks and mouth and everywhere, starved for him.

I clawed off his shirt. He kicked off his boots and they sank to the floor. Only our heads were above water now, our embrace buoyant. I was light in his arms, and he could easily shift me into position to bite at my nipples.

I moaned, my arm flailing toward the edge of the pool. My ragged nails tried to clutch at the slick tiles, only to slip away. I grabbed his shoulders instead. Feeling his skin bare and wet felt right to me in some primal way, like he was becoming more a part of my world as I became part of his. And the unrelenting attention of his mouth was driving me to madness.

"Wrin, I need you."

"I need you, too."

I tore the buttons of his trousers and pulled out his cock, stroking it to see his eyes slightly glaze. I could feel its hard thickness under my hand and my body craved him inside me.

"Show me how to do it," he said.

I laughed. "Gods, I hardly know myself, but it can't be very different. The mers would say that your horn goes in my cave. We'll figure it out."

Indeed, we certainly did.

Chapter Twenty-Two

T<small>ALWYN</small>

O<small>H</small>, but then the weather started turning cold. Cursed November. Wrindel was far too cold to climb in the pool with me. He had to find an elemental mage who could warm the waters for me every day, even though I was much heartier against cold than an elf, but the pool could freeze over without intervention. Rusa and King Lefior's love affair had spanned spring to fall —maybe winter had broken them up as surely as anything else.

Still, we married that month, in a ceremony in the Hall of Marble Pools that was attended by everyone in the kingdom and all their cousins, or so it seemed to me. I could spend a little time out of water, and I did, wearing a long gown and a headdress of pearls, sitting on a stool so we could say our vows.

I felt the weight of the silk gown I wore, covering my tail. I saw Kiara and a few other girls watching me with sour expressions. Violinists played beautiful, celebratory music in the background but I couldn't help but think that other royal weddings were not like this one.

For one thing, I had no family in attendance. My sisters

wanted to come, but I forbade them. I didn't want them to see that I didn't fit in. I worried that some of the elves would snub them.

Then, we had to alter the ceremony because I couldn't walk in. It was hard not to feel self-conscious and fret over what my presence would mean for the rest of Wrin's life.

Wrindel slipped a silver ring on my finger, formed like a small crown of vines with tiny leaves.

"I vow to honor you and protect you for all of my days," he said. "I pray to the gods that you shall only know good luck and happiness, but I swear that no man or misfortune will tear us asunder. Through spring and summer, autumn and winter, you are my one and only, Talwyn Silverfin."

Then he leaned over to me and whispered in my ear, "And I vow not to take any crap over this, nor allow you to do so."

I couldn't help but laugh, and my vows came easier then. I knew I didn't make a conventional princess, but I was pleasantly surprised when we adjourned to the banquet and many ladies and gentlemen of the court welcomed me and thanked me for helping to save the king, and after our wedding I felt a little less shy at spending time in the Hall of Marble Pools or the moat where people could see me. Visitors from abroad always wanted a glimpse of me; a mermaid princess taking a swim in the palace moat was something quite notable apparently.

Our original plan for me to only spend the mating season with Wrindel was quickly abandoned. Wrindel's room was being remodeled with an extension to the balcony pool so I could sleep near him.

But I still wanted legs. Gods, I wanted them! I think the Great Temptation burned in me worse than ever. I wanted to be free to roam the palace and the town and the world beyond. I wanted to stroll gardens and ride horses. I wanted Wrindel to part my legs and do all the things he used to do to me. I knew we must be happier than Rusa and King Lefior, but—sometimes I poked at Rusa's jewelry and couldn't bear that she had done this to me. Given me a taste of legs, and then taken them away forever.

This was it. This was my life and I knew I just had to accept its joys and not wish for more, but wishing for more was how I had always lived.

I was spending a lot of time with Ellara, who had taken over my reading lessons for the most part. She told me all the court gossip and became the ear for all my frustrations so I didn't lose my mind. Besides that, as soon as the curse was broken, Ellara got pregnant herself. We talked of babies for hours, chided ourselves for being so boring as to talk of babies for hours, and then talked of them for hours more. My pregnancy was starting to show; I could feel my child kicking.

I never, ever spoke of the possibility that something bad might happen. I couldn't bear it. I needed to know that he or she would be a child of the surface world. Gods, even if my baby was a mer, I wasn't sure I could stand it. It was one thing for me to choose this life for myself, but it seemed such a cruel way to grow up. I desperately wanted someone to assure me that the children of mermaids and land folk were likely to have legs. I kept pestering every foreign dignitary who wanted to see me swimming in the moat, hoping someone would know a mermaid bride, all through the winter, into the spring. I heard rumors. Plenty of rumors, gone stale with centuries. Nothing I could cling to.

One day I happened to ask one of these foreign dignitaries while I was wearing Rusa's bracelets.

He looked at me with shock and walked over, giving me a slight bow. "How do you speak Alimandan?"

"I—I don't."

"You're speaking it now."

"No, you're speaking elvish!"

He laughed. "You must have some magic that takes away the barriers of language. I have heard of this."

"My bracelets belonged to a witch..."

"Ah, yes. They make these bracelets to use on the spice roads for trading. This is rare magic. Don't waste it on me. I don't know anything of mermaids. The spell will not last forever."

I was still thinking of it later, when Ellara and I were reading an old book of merfolk legends, and suddenly I thought of something. "Ellara...the old book from the archives with the pictures of mermaids...the one that's written in elvish script but in an ancient language... Do you think if you read the word aloud while I wore the bracelets, I might understand them?"

"It couldn't hurt!" She looked excited. She was back with the book so quickly that I said, "I hope you didn't dash up and down the stairs, as pregnant as you are."

"You're more pregnant than me."

"Well, where am *I* going?"

She carefully opened the pages, and opened them to the pictures of the mermaid being taken by the man on the shore.

"A mer...maid...," she said, reading very slowly as she sounded out the words.

I shrieked with excitement. Ellara jumped and clutched her heart. "It's working, then? It sounds like gibberish to me."

"You just said 'a mermaid'! Go on. Keep reading!"

She read slowly, but the answers soon unfolded for me, the first bit of true hope I had felt in these many months.

A mermaid can become a creature of the land, and bear a child with men, but it is not easy magic. It is a custom in some areas of the world for a young mermaid to be offered to a human chieftain as a bride, whether she wishes it or not. She must swallow a shore-stone and then he must take the shore-stone from her. This will give her legs forever and she will be as beautiful as any woman who ever walked the earth, but she will lose her memories and if she ever lays eyes on the stone, she is likely to steal it back and abandon her husband and children. Her children are likely to be sickly. The other path is harder still, for it requires true trust and love between a man and his bride...

Chapter Twenty-Three

WRINDEL

"NGAAAH...!" In the wave of a painful contraction, Talwyn scraped my bare leg. I had rolled up my trousers and was trying to help as best I could, but she had mostly been clawing at me and squeezing my hands off. "Just get it over with already!" she snapped at her own belly.

"It'll be over soon," I said, trying my best to soothe her. I don't think I was much use at this point.

She slumped into the water for a moment, just her hands still remaining above the surface, now clenching the edge of the pool.

The royal midwife hovered in the background, looking calm but staying out of it. She was a kind woman who seemed to genuinely like Talwyn, but she had been very uncomfortable examining her. I think she was just praying nothing bad happened. Talwyn had spoken to a mermaid midwife about what to expect, but the woman wouldn't come to the palace. Ellara was there too, and had been fetching water and towels all through the night since Talwyn first went into labor.

I don't think it was only pain that had Talwyn clawing at me and screaming. The stakes were so high that I had been drinking a little too much ale this evening myself.

According to the book, there was a proper way to make a mermaid your bride. First, she had to activate the magic of the shore-stone. Then, the man must take the shore-stone. A child must be conceived. And then, the man must return the shore-stone to her, restore her memories, and claim her once more in her true form.

Only this, the book said, would seal the bonds of love and trust to a sufficient degree that she could become a part of her lover's world forever.

By pure accident, we had done everything right.

"Hardly by accident," Talwyn said at the time. "It makes perfect sense. It was the right way to treat someone you love, that's all."

But putting all our trust in a thousand-year-old book was all we could lean on, and it still didn't give all the details we wanted. Would our child be healthy? Was Talwyn going to get her legs back? If the book was wrong, it was wrong, and that would be that. The lack of surety or having any control over our fate was making us both a little crazy.

We would love this child no matter what it was, but there was nothing we could do if it couldn't survive. And if that happened, we could never dare to try again.

"It's coming..." She gripped my hand and then looked at me plaintively. "Oh, Wrin, here we go...please tell me it will be all right."

"It'll be all right, sunshine."

She gripped both my hands, screaming as she pushed. Her tail thrashed and her face turned bright red. Ellara covered her eyes.

"Try to breathe," the midwife urged.

"Should she come out of the water so we can see what's happening?" Ellara asked, slowly lowering her hands, looking pale and very pregnant herself. She had wanted to help, but I wondered if it was such a good idea.

Talwyn's eyes opened wide and she pulled away from me.

"Something's happening..." She sounded scared. I thought my heart might bloody well stop. I jumped into the water with her, instantly soaking my clothes, and tried to hold her.

She flailed, and kicked me. At least it felt that way. And then I saw—it was true. Her tail had split into legs. Her scream now was absolutely bloodcurdling. "What's happening to me? It hurts..."

"You have *legs*."

She started sobbing in a choked way.

"Get her to the bed," the midwife said.

"No—no, I still want to be in the water...please..." She pushed again, and I saw a head starting to emerge, past all the bubbles kicked up by our commotion. Ellara had walked right up to the edge of the pool.

"Talwyn, I can see it! You're doing great!" she said.

Another push, another scream—Ithrin knocked on the door and was ignored by everyone—and I tried to catch the infant in my hands but the baby was born screaming—and swimming. Talwyn seemed ready for this and caught the wriggling little creature in her hands.

Our child was a mer.

Chapter Twenty-Four

Talwyn

When I saw her, I started crying with some relief and a good dose of complete despair. The midwife rushed over to help. Now that the baby was out, she seemed to know what to do, cutting the cord and cleaning her off. "You should get into bed so I can examine you," she said, but I hardly paid attention. I looked at my little girl, stroking the fine layer of fair hair on her head. She looked elven.

"Is it a girl or a boy?" Wrindel asked, in a preternaturally calm voice.

"A girl...the easiest way to tell is that males have a small extra fin at the base of their tail."

"She looks healthy," he said. Her tail already felt strong, her fins flopping as she let out little furious cries.

I sobbed again, utterly exhausted and weak, blood clouding the water. "My legs, Wrin... I can't change back. I don't understand what happened..."

"It must have something to do with the magic. Like the book

said, if you conceive a child while you have legs, you can become a part of this world forever."

"She—she *can't* grow up as a mermaid if neither of us are merfolk! I can't consign my baby to a life inside of a tiny pool..." I started bawling. Gods, I just felt broken. After all the build up, all the worry...I realized how much I had expected a baby with legs. I wasn't supposed to be the one who got legs out of this. What could I do? Find her a mer-family to foster her? Maybe one of my sisters would raise her?

But she was *ours*. I didn't want to give her up. But now it seemed I was human.

I felt like the gods had just played a huge trick on me.

Ellara and the midwife both seemed speechless. Damn it all, I knew everyone expected a new elven prince or princess.

Wrin, my poor soaking wet and shivering Wrin, cradled my head against his chest. "Can I hold her?" he asked.

"Of—of course..."

I passed her into his arms.

As the baby left my touch and was swept into her elven father's embrace, fully out of the water, a miracle happened before my eyes. Her tail split into legs. She started kicking and screaming now.

"Talwyn—look—"

"I see!"

Ellara gasped. "Legs!" she cried.

"Does that mean she'll be a mermaid whenever I hold her, and an elf whenever you hold her?" I asked, which was horrifying in another way.

"Let's see."

"I'm almost afraid to touch her now..." But when I took her back, she kept her legs. It was only when I lowered her back into the water that she changed into a mermaid again. And then, back to legs when Wrindel pulled her out. She started screaming her little head off.

"She's both," I marveled. "It's—it's perfect."

"I don't she likes changing," he said with a laugh. "Come on, let's get you both into the bed."

Ellara took the baby and toweled her off, gushing over her little toes, while Wrindel toweled *me* off and helped me into a shift. My legs felt newborn again, and I was deeply sore and utterly exhausted. Still, it was such a happy time, now that I knew it had all worked out. I could hardly believe that I was human again, and so was she.

I woke up a little later, groggy and disoriented. My baby was in her crib right beside my bed, swaddled and sleeping. Ellara was on the other side of the room at the breakfast table, setting out a spread.

"The menfolk are celebrating with a little honey wine," Ellara said. "You'd better wake up if you don't like the name Melitara. Wrindel wants to name her after his late mother. Ithrin was planning naming two girls after his mother and sister, but yours *did* come first. They're arguing over it now."

"You know, if they can work it out amongst themselves, it's fine with me," I said. "It's a nice name. I know how important the late family is to them. I never thought of what to call her. I was...superstitious about it, I guess."

"She's beautiful," Ellara said, looking into the crib.

"She's very small..." It made me nervous to be responsible for such a helpless little thing.

"Babies typically *are* small," Ellara said.

"Read up on that, did you?" I teased her. She was always starting sentences with "I read in one of the baby books..." I was still struggling with the words a bit, although improving. Wrindel said he didn't take to reading easily either.

"Our little ones are going to be almost as close in age as twins." She handed me a cup of coffee. "I put a lot of milk in it because I don't know if you should drink that while you're nursing. I guess I'd better find out, shouldn't I?"

"I'm drinking it anyway." I sighed, throwing off the covers. I still wasn't used to being smothered in cloth. I looked at my feet and slowly flexed my toes. Then I looked at little possibly-Melitara. "I envy her. She can change back. I guess you have to be born of both worlds to exist in both worlds."

"It's the magic of love," Ellara said dreamily. "I told you."

"You're such a romantic."

"I have turned into one, haven't I? I wasn't always. But I'm still a naughty goblin—hold on." She waved a finger at me and crossed the room, rummaging in a bag. "By the way, I almost threw up when you were having the baby. It probably doesn't bode well for me."

"Oh yes, I saw you covering your eyes over there."

"I didn't think I was squeamish, but...when your tail split into legs, at first I thought the baby *broke* you."

"You and me both."

"The goblin queen, Sabela? She sent me this healing stone when she heard I was pregnant..." She took out a smooth white stone that could only be described as...phallic. "It's a goblin spell. Actually, a faery spell. Those faeries, my goodness! The stories I've heard about *them*. But—the goblins and the faeries trade a lot. It heals you up after pregnancy very fast. Of course, first you are only going to think about feeling better. But it'll also help shorten the time for you to...get back to business with Wrindel, you know. She sent it to me, but I think you should have it."

After she left, with considerable trepidation, I slid the stone inside me. I was braced for it to hurt, but it was actually soothing and warm and felt really wonderful—and vaguely arousing. I nursed Melitara and fell into the sleep of ages—until she started crying again.

The next several days were much the same and we weren't alone enough to do anything, but I must say I rather enjoyed them. I finally felt like a proper princess, laying in bed with my newborn, sleeping as much as I could, with no responsibilities whatsoever. Occasionally a maid would come and spruce up my hair and offer me a robe so I could show her off to members of the court. I was also appointed a nurse for the baby, a very kind woman around fifty years of age—young for an elf—who had once been a nurse for Wrin.

Best of all, my sisters came to the court for the first time. Wrindel and Ithrin met them at the shore and brought them to my room, and we all tried to give Melitara a bath. She hated it. Her screams were unrelenting. At least for now, Melitara liked legs better, but maybe she was just used to them. I knew how that felt.

Allie and Mirella were still delighted. They loved the palace and gushed over little Mellie despite her crying.

"Just think, Arlion and I might have one of our own in another couple of years!" Mirella said, to my horror. I had to remind myself that even Mirella was almost eighteen now.

I embarrassed myself by sobbing when they had to go, but soon I would be able to walk to the shore and visit them and show Mellie her other home.

Finally, a calm afternoon fell, the nurse was taking the baby out for a stroll in the garden, and the healing stone seemed to have done a miraculous job of putting my poor body back to rights. When Wrindel came in from an evening card game with Ithrin, I was waiting for him wearing nothing but stockings.

Chapter Twenty-Five

Wrindel

I swung open the door, shrugging off my jacket, and stopped short when I saw Talwyn spread out on the bed, almost entirely naked, her breasts full and luscious, her belly still a little rounded from carrying our child. In recent months I had noticed, despite the pregnancy, that her once tanned skin had grown pale and she wasn't as strong as she once was.

But right now, she had never looked so content and fertile and I could see the sunlight coming back into her eyes, the bright future ahead of us. Soon, I would teach her to ride and take her all over the countryside.

"Talwyn...gods. Isn't it too soon? I don't know much about these things..."

"Ellara gave me a little faery trick to help with that, a healing stone that goes inside me. It's been healing me right up and it works very well. It also has been reminding me constantly how good it's going to feel to have you inside me again... It's made me feel so open and ready for you. Take off your trousers."

My cock was already painfully hard, but I didn't obey her

right away. Instead I slid onto the bed beside her, grabbed her wrists and pinned them to the sheets, kissing her roughly.

"Is it still inside you now?" I asked.

"Yes..."

"Good." I kept her hands pinned so she couldn't do anything about it, but now I crossed her wrists just behind her head and held them with one of mine. I fondled her heavy breasts until she was panting hard. I bit her nipples, tasting drops of her sweet milk, but then I left them alone so there would be milk enough for Mellie.

I slipped my fingers between her folds, finding the base of the healing stone, a warm hard shaft inside her.

"Should I be jealous?"

"It's not as big as you," she said.

I pulled it out to see its size. "A little faery trick, huh? Not *so* little." I shoved it back inside her and felt her stiffen at the invasion. I hoped I hadn't been too rough—but then I saw her mouth fall open and her eyes hood with pleasure and knew I had not. My girl was ready for anything by now.

"Please, Wrin, it's just a tease," she said. "It stirs my senses without satisfying anything."

"You need satisfaction, sunshine?"

"Yes...yes. Don't take too long. I don't know how long Hanaria will be gone with Mellie."

I let go of her hands, spread her gorgeous legs, and sucked on her clit.

"Oh gods..."

"You missed this, didn't you?"

"More than I wanted to admit!"

I licked and sucked on her clit with complete focus, deciding that this was no time to keep her waiting long. She was so wet and ripe. The spring strawberries could not have tasted sweeter than she did, but even sweeter was the way she writhed and let out shuddering gasps.

"More, please...," she said.

"You really are the girl of my dreams, aren't you?"

"I'd better be, after all we've been through."

"But I still haven't had all of you, sunshine. I want to fuck that sweet little ass of yours. While that stone is inside you, filling you up everywhere."

She blushed so deeply that it tested all my willpower.

"You want to know how it feels, don't you?" I spoke softly in her ear.

"I do." She nibbled her nail. "It won't hurt?"

"What happened the last time you asked that question?"

"Nothing bad."

"Exactly."

Chapter Twenty-Six

Talwyn

Wrindel put his hands on my hips and rolled me over, just stroking my bare bottom for a moment. I was still nervous that the nursemaid might return, but I was also nervous for what he was about to do, so I let him caress me. It felt so good to have legs again, even though they didn't feel quite right. The skin was so exquisitely sensitive. In some ways, I hope I never got entirely used to having legs. It made his touch all the more stimulating.

Gently, he slipped a hand under my pelvis and pulled me up so I was kneeling on the bed, my ass in the air. I could feel his anticipation and it made me want it more. I could hear his breath quicken with excitement. He opened a drawer and took out a bottle of oil.

"You're so perfect, Tal," he said. "Since the day I saw you."

"I'm just so glad I'm...human again."

"I'm glad you don't have to live like a decorative fish in a pond," he said. "And yes, I'm glad that it's so much easier for us to give each other pleasure this way. But you've never been less than perfect to me."

"I know." I swallowed down a lump of joy threatening to become tears. "But get on with it already. The nursemaid!"

He tugged my ass back against his pelvis and cupped my dangling breasts. "The door has a lock." I could feel the healing stone teasing against my inner walls, building up my arousal, and slowly ground my ass against him, feeling it inside me like an itch being scratched.

He slicked his cock with the lubricant and spread my knees apart a little farther on the bed, so I was at the right level. In another moment I felt the head press against my nether hole. It was a strange sensation, but he had already been preparing me for this. I was used to his fingers there, just not something as thick as his cock. And at the same time, the healing stone was already filling me, but not nearly enough. I craved something more. I wanted to satisfy him in every way, and I trusted him that he would never hurt me. He pushed farther, and I forced myself to relax, as I knew I must not tense my muscles if I was going to take him.

Gods, I felt so full. I groaned as he impaled me.

"Beautiful, sunshine. Your ass is a work of art like the rest of you."

He reached down and pumped the healing stone in and out of me, and once he had found a rhythm there, he started to work his cock in and out of my ass. First one and then the other. My weak legs were trembling, but I forced myself to keep them up. I could do nothing else. This was too much. I was completely at his mercy now. I felt used in the best sort of way.

The orgasm built up almost stealthily. In my warm haze of satisfaction it almost seemed impossible that the climb would ever end. The unrelenting friction, his other hand touching me gently, my shuddering little body...suddenly it was like thunder rumbling out from the clouds. I felt a mounting spark of unbearable lust that now built rapidly until I thought I would die!

I was splitting open for him, crying as the most overwhelming orgasm I had ever had pounded through my body. "Wrin—stop! Gods, no, don't stop—" I didn't even know what I wanted at first. His hand stopped working the healing stone, and he just fucked me hard. The last vestiges of my orgasm were still rippling through me as he came. It must not have been long, but it felt three times longer than any climax I'd ever had.

When I collapsed, he stripped off my stockings and carried me into the pool of water. The warm water felt wonderful on my skin. I spread my naked limbs and let the soft caress of the water soothe me.

"My mermaid," he said.

"Not anymore..."

"You will always be my mermaid," he said.

"I wonder how Melitara will feel as she grows up," I said. "What if she wanted to live under the water?"

"I think it's a little early to worry about that. We might as well wonder, what if she wants to join a traveling theater troupe?"

"I suppose you're right..."

"She's a princess of Wyndyr. She will have responsibilities to her people, as I do. It's just a part of being born into royalty. You never starve or suffer, but you have to follow certain protocol. You can marry anyone you like in Wyndyr, we've proved that. But you also have to be ready to inherit the throne."

"Girls too?"

"Oh yes, there is a long tradition of elven queens." He reached for a bar of soap sitting on the edge of the pool. "Now, it's true, we still generally maintain that the eldest son is the heir, but we've made concessions when the daughter is more...shall we say...up to the task? Sometimes the men can be pretty irresponsible..."

"I don't believe that. Surely you have never done anything irresponsible," I said, giving him an innocent face.

He grinned. "Well, I'm managing the husband-and-father part, but I'm glad I don't have to be king. Ithrin and all his meetings and bookkeeping..."

"May he live long," I said.

"He enjoys it," Wrindel said. "It's the parties *he* hates. This city needs two kings."

After all the frenzied lovemaking of moments before, now he

started to wash my hair, which was every bit as nice. Except for the maids rushing in to briefly fuss with me, I had not really been taking this sort of care of myself.

In the midst of this, I heard the approaching screams of an infant, and we exchanged a grim, tired smile. Wrin started to leave the pool, and I touched his arm.

"Keep doing what you're doing," I said. "Let's have Hanaria drop her off right here. It's never too early for a mermaid to learn to swim."

THANK YOU FOR READING! If you enjoyed this book, I would be much obliged if you consider leaving a review. And to make sure you don't miss a release, sign up for my mailing list, and come chat with me on Facebook! Is there a fairy tale you'd like to see? Drop me a line on Facebook or at lidiyafoxglove@lidiyafoxglove.com! As I write this, the season is turning to the great controversial topic: pumpkin spice, love it or hate it? And next up are books for the holidays. Gretel will be encounter a wicked faery chocolatier for an extra-naughty All Hallow's Eve story, and then our Little Red Riding Hood, Fersa, will meet her long lost human father's family for one of those awkward Christmases. You know the topics you should avoid for Christmas dinner: politics, religion, and wolves in heat.

Fairy Tale Heat Series

Every book is standalone and can be read in any order, although some characters might pop up in later books!

About the Author

Lidiya Foxglove has always loved a good fairy tale, whether it's sweet or steamy, and she likes to throw in a little of both. Sometimes she thinks she ought to do something other than reading and writing, but that would require doing more laundry. So...never mind.

lidiyafoxglove@lidiyafoxglove.com

Made in the USA
Monee, IL
30 November 2021

83522807R00094